Zeustian Logic

Sabrina Malcolm

GECKO PRESS

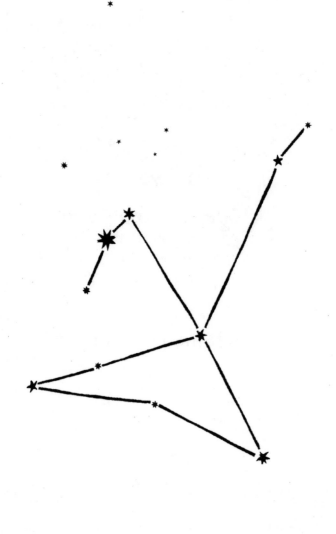

when he shall die
Take him and cut him out in little stars
And he will make the face of heav'n so fine
That all the world will be in love with night
And pay no worship to the garish sun.
— WILLIAM SHAKESPEARE, *ROMEO AND JULIET*

Aquila the Eagle

Okay, so—imagine you're an ordinary bloke in ancient Greece. A shepherd, in fact. And maybe you're pretty good-looking, at least according to your girlfriend down at the shearing shed.

One morning, just on sunrise, you're in the hills herding sheep, as shepherds do, and suddenly the sky goes dark and there's a huge blast of air, and a honking great eagle swoops down and grabs you in its talons and yanks you into the sky.

Now imagine the eagle flies straight up and you're cold and the Earth is far, far below and getting farther, so everything looks *very*, *very small*, and you can barely breathe and you're thinking, What the hell, and then the eagle drops you in a place called Mount Olympus, which turns out to be where Zeus lives.

And you're given the job of "cup bearer to the gods".

That's right: the gods like the look of you, so they're letting you cart their mead around. You get to be, essentially, the ancient Greek equivalent of a drinks trolley.

I like the randomness of Greek mythology. Later, Zeus put the shepherd up in the sky as the constellation Aquarius.

It was a bit of a habit with Zeus, putting stuff in the sky.

I don't remember this because it was before I was born, but in the 1970s, NASA's Pioneer 11 space probe zoomed past Saturn and Jupiter, taking pictures and sending them back to Earth. After that, the probe just kept going.

And—here's a nice connection with the shepherd-stealing eagle—in four million years' time, give or take, Pioneer 11 will fly past Lambda Aquilae, which is the sixth brightest star in the Eagle constellation (and, incidentally, the 270th brightest star in the sky).

Mind you, NASA won't know anything about it (that's assuming NASA still exists, which is unlikely but you never know), because for a long time now the probe hasn't had enough power to transmit anything back to Earth. It's on its own out there.

Is it just me, or is that fairly sad and tragic?

There's a mental picture I have of Dad, alone like that space probe, on the mountain with the wind screaming around and snow covering him and sometimes, I guess, uncovering him. Wherever he is.

It's not one of my best-loved images. In fact it's worse than lousy, but I don't suppose I'll ever get rid of it.

It's a strange thing, having a famous father who's dead.

For most of my life, my father was a genius. Everyone said it—internet, TV, random strangers. Climbing sites called him a luminary, a natural, a brilliant climber with legendary stamina.

He went up and down Everest and K2 half a dozen times each, but what made him more famous were the trips in between, when he figured out radical new routes on lower but harder peaks.

When he got into mountain guiding, the bloggers loved that too, saying it was another step in his stellar career.

I remember one time when the local paper called him the Prince of Peaks. Dad read out the article in the kitchen, waving his arm for emphasis, but he was laughing and the newspaper was crackling so much that Mum had to grab it and start again so we could hear what he'd actually said.

After that, every now and then Mum would stop what she was doing, raise her fist and yell, "Hero of the Hills!" or "Star of the Slopes!" or "King of Climbers!"

She thought it was hilarious.

Then, 356 days ago at 2.00 p.m. Nepal Standard Time, my father and one of his clients decided to abandon their summit attempt and go back down the mountain.

No one really knows what happened after that. Later, searchers found the client—dead. But Dad's still there. Somewhere.

Figaro the Cat

If Zeus's eagle came for Boyd from next door, I wouldn't mind. It could take his idiot car, too. Zeus could shove them up in the sky, for all I care.

Boyd used to be an okay kind of guy, if you don't mind diehard obsessive football mania, but then he turned sixteen and his parents (get this) *gave* him a car and instantly he turned into the world's biggest tool. From that moment on, he's been either under the car, tinkering with the springs or muffler, or—having passed his driving tests freakishly fast—hooning around the streets making psychotic amounts of noise.

("Hooning" is Mrs Ziegler's word. An oldie but a goody, she says. And "splendidly onomatopoeic". She's like that—she almost salivates over unusual words. It's probably a good quality in an English teacher.)

Actually, I couldn't give a toss about Boyd, except that every time there's a clear night for star viewing and I set up the telescope in the only dark corner of our garden, he chooses that night to head out to the garage, flick on every light in the place and mess around for hours with the car. Which stuffs up my chances of viewing anything fainter than the moon. Not to mention the crappy smoke his car belches out, which also wrecks star viewing. Admittedly, he's got help there from a few billion other people. But at least most of them use their cars to get somewhere useful.

Dozo. (Dozo—also from Mrs Ziegler. Also apt. Clearly, I was born in the wrong era.)

It really puzzles me how two people from the same family (sort of) can be so different. Boyd, for instance, has a half-sister named Phoebe who seems perfectly all right. You wouldn't think they shared one gene, even.

It might not actually be such a good thing, Boyd and his car hanging around in the sky. I'm pretty sure he's got a grudge against me. Lately he's been giving me some seriously sneery looks. Maybe he's picked up on my less-than-flattering opinion of him and the idiot-mobile.

But I have to watch myself. He's a couple of years older than me and has bigger muscles. If you've got a frame that's average-sized or slightly less, you can't just ignore stuff like that.

My friend Attila says I should ask Boyd about the grudge.

"You live next door, yes?" he said around a baked-bean sandwich. (And he makes his own lunches. Figure that out.) "So. Plenty of chances to chat."

"Right," I said.

"So. Y'just go up to him," he said. "And y'just ask." Then, in case I hadn't grasped the concept, he demonstrated. "'Hey. You got a grudge against me?'"

"Right," I said.

"And then—" he spread his non-sandwich hand wide— "you'll know." He shrugged. "Where's the problem?"

Right.

Just getting back to having a dead father. One of the things about it is this.

Anyone who *doesn't* have one doesn't know about all the days, and nights, when you're wiped out by it, flattened, and the weeks and months when things slowly get a tiny bit better (but even then with major setbacks), and then one day you feel just slightly okay so you crack a smile, and everyone looks shocked, like you're evil.

If someone in your family dies, you can get counselling to help you cope. But no one counsels other people how to talk to you.

Attila would say that's a niche in the market for someone.

A few weeks after the memorial service, Mum took Fen and me to see a grief counsellor, an oldish guy who told us to write letters.

"This might sound a little strange," he said. "And I apologize if it's in any way upsetting. But I'd like you to think about writing a letter to your father."

I thought, What the?

"I can see you're surprised," said the counsellor. "And that's perfectly normal. The idea is just this. Tell him how much you miss him. Tell him what you've been thinking. What you've been doing. That sort of thing. Just—write him a letter."

I thought, *What the?*

"It might not seem like it now, but you'll find it helps, in the long run."

"How do we know it's helped," I said, kind of quietly, "if we can't clone ourselves?"

"Pardon?" said the counsellor.

"Tuttle," said Mum.

6

"No, that's all right," said the counsellor. "What was that, Duncan—uh, Tuttle?"

"How do we know it's working if we can't make two of ourselves and get one to do the letter and one to *not* do the letter?"

"Tuttle," said Mum.

Things went quiet.

"Let's just do the letter and see what happens, shall we?" said the counsellor.

I didn't do the letter. We went to see the guy a few more times, and he asked about it once or twice but then gave up.

I wonder, sometimes, if Fen ever wrote a letter. He doesn't talk much. Mostly he stays in his room. I think he's reading. The pile of books outside his door gets moved around, so that's a clue, but I hardly see him. Well—he goes to school, obviously, but other than that, for the last year he's been a pale, sick-looking seven-year-old zombie presence.

Just lately I've been getting him off to bed at night because Mum's stopped doing it. I tell him the occasional story, and he seems okay with that. But he's really not what you'd call talkative.

He used to be a total chatterbox. He'd rush inside, jabbering about something Figaro had done, and drag me out to see, still talking non-stop. When he was upset he was just as gabby, but at the top of his voice. Our after-school sessions at the library always—*always*—involved at least one intensely humiliating incident because, as everyone knows, teenagers hate being the focus of attention. Unless it's their idea.

Whereas Fen didn't care. I remember one time he ran, squeak-shouting, all the way from the kids' section to where I was browsing in Young Adults.

7

"Tutter! Tutter! *The Sword in the Stone*! You'll read it to me? Yowsa, Tutter!"

He did know libraries were supposed to be quiet. He just forgot. Every time.

"Yowsa" was one of Dad's sayings. There was also "Who you gonna call?" and "Make it so." And "I'll be back," which he always drawled, in a bad imitation of Arnold Schwarzenegger, when he left for a mountain. "I'll be back" even featured in one of those mountaineering magazines, when they did a big piece on Dad a couple of years ago.

Figaro, by the way, is the pet cat of the people on our non-Boyd side. His owners are quieter than mice and practically invisible, but Figaro is loud and psychotic. He has a trick where he crouches down in front of you and waggles his butt, then he catapults from ground level onto your chest. You have to be ready for it, because he expects you to catch him. Then he puts his front paws either side of your neck and gets smoochy all over your face.

That's if he's in a good mood. If he's feeling surly, he skulks in the flowers and ambushes your ankles. Or he lies on his back on the driveway, yowling and clawing at the air, then suddenly hurtles vertically off the ground in a savage attack on a passing fly. I think he's got the cat version of ADHD.

These days, I choose Fen's library books myself. I don't know if I'm getting the right ones—I just try to guess how his year-ago tastes might have changed. I put the books outside his door and take away the old ones.

Every day or two, the stack changes shape.

I figure that's good.

Aquarius the Water Carrier

Every year in April and May there's a meteor shower called the Eta Aquarids that looks like it's shooting out of the mouth of Aquarius's pitcher.

I saw it this morning and it was spectacular. Even worth getting up at 5 a.m. for. I'd have gone back inside for Fen, but he's even less of a morning person than I am.

I'd only been outside half a minute, stamping around in the dark and blowing clouds of breath, when a streak of light shot down the sky. And another one. It was like some superhero athlete was doing javelin practice. Maybe with a little kid superhero tagging along—one who had a tiny javelin of his own but wasn't that good. There'd be sudden long, bright flashes that flared halfway to the horizon, and then little flashes and pops that fizzed out, then more long ones.

Impressive.

Here's another good thing about the Eta Aquarids: the southern hemisphere's the best place to see them. Those poor suckers in the north only get to see about ten meteors an hour. Here in New Zealand we get thirty.

After breakfast and lunchboxes and teeth and the last-minute stampede at the door, I clanged the gate shut and slowed down to a shuffle beside our fence, paddling through my bag and trying to remember if I'd put my science book in.

Fen trotted ahead. I glanced up after him, and remembered when he first started school.

In those first few weeks, Dad used to walk with us. Outside our gate, he'd hoist Fen up to his shoulders, grip his legs and growl, "Y'ready?"

Fen would yell, "Yeah!"

Then Dad would take off down the path with crazy loping steps, zig-zagging from side to side making engine noises. It was violently embarrassing and I always trailed a long way behind, agonizing about the ammunition it would give Boyd if he saw us, but Fen loved it. He craned backwards and sideways, shrieking and giggling and grabbing at branches, knowing Dad had a cast-iron grip on his legs.

Boyd's car was in their driveway.

Sometimes in the mornings Boyd has a quick tinker with the idiot-mobile. He's always one of the last to arrive at school, whipping up the driveway with a volley of pointless gear changes—not quite burning rubber or he'd get a detention, but fast enough for a few menacing looks from teachers.

I burrowed deeper in my bag, feeling for the corners of the textbook.

Something metal thumped on concrete, and Boyd himself scuffled out from underneath the car. He was in his camo shorts and old Nissan tee-shirt, and the tool belt that's his pride and joy. He gave me a sneery look.

Obviously, I didn't sneer back. But I thought sneery thoughts.

Boyd's mate Derek was lounging on a toolbox lid on the lawn, picking grass in the sunlight. His life's role seems to be to slouch around looking intense.

Keeping up his disgusted lip curl, Boyd grabbed an adjustable wrench and pulled himself back under the car.

I think it surprised us both when I said, "D'you ever worry about global warming?"

My voice even went a bit tweety at the end. Very smooth.

There was a pause. A blackbird whistled. Boyd hauled himself by his forearms, slowly, from under the car.

One of the unsettling things about Boyd is his invisible eyebrows—his pale-orange hair doesn't show up against his skin. Now even his eyes had disappeared in a frown. He uncurled and stood up in one move, and in a couple of steps he was right there, an oily rag swinging from his hand.

He's taller than me, so I had to look up.

"The hell?" he said. I felt the puff of air. Beyond the glare of the windshield Derek leaned over, watching.

"The exhaust crap from your car," I said. "It stuffs up the air."

Incredulous disgust grew on Boyd's face. "What's my car got to do with you?" He leaned at me, and a concerned corner of my mind registered the size of his arms. "What's a loser like you," he added, "know about my car?"

In my peripheral vision Derek craned further.

Boyd answered himself. "Nothin'. Y'know nothin' about it."

He leaned further, twisted, and crunched me with his shoulder. I blundered back a few steps and caught my balance.

My forehead went hot. It's always a bad sign.

"I can see why you need the tool belt," I said.

With another step he loomed over me like a curling wave.

"A belt," I said from under the wave, "for a tool."

He seemed to swell up in front of me.

A blue car slid into view at the corner. The people inside were looking out their side windows, studying the *For Sale* house a couple of doors down. Boyd heard the engine and turned.

The people were still gawking, the car still gliding along.

Boyd swung back. I ducked, but recovered.

He snorted. "A mouse. Aren't you?"

Over his shoulder he said casually, like he was talking to the people in the car drifting past, "A cowardy mouse. Just like your famous dad."

But he made sure he turned back, so he could see my face.

The Black Tortoise
of the North

If karma's real, someone in our family must have ransacked a lot of villages in a previous life. What else explains the butthead-next-door we're lumbered with now?

From the end of our street I looked down through the trees to the bus shelter across the road, where Attila should be loitering. I wanted a rant. And he'd be sympathetic—he thinks even less of Boyd than I do. Then I realized it was Thursday and he'd have gone early, for underwater hockey.

Fen was at the bottom of the steps, waiting to cross the road with me. When we got across he glanced in my direction for about a millisecond—the closest he gets to saying goodbye these days—and plodded to where Mrs Conrad was waiting in her usual spot. She gave me the wave and thumbs-up that demonstrates she's got the hand-over, and led Fen around the corner to the primary school, chatting at his lowered head.

Getting on the bus didn't improve my mood. Usually, talking to Attila drowns out the witless bleating of the thirteen-year-olds, a.k.a. newbs, but today I was at their mercy. I stared out the window and finally slid into a daydream of a food fight between Zeus and a bunch of Titans.

At school Attila was in the library corridor, jittery and damp from the pool, and he started talking as soon as he saw me. The bell rang and the usual bedlam erupted, and even though I couldn't hear a word Attila was saying, somehow his waving arms and unintelligible yelling and the annoying specks of water flicking off his hair all helped push Boyd into the background.

In English we started our Chosen Novel project. Except (as Attila pointed out to Mrs Ziegler) they're not *chosen*, because we had to pick from a list. Also (he pointed this out too), every single one of them looked as boring as the inside of a paper bag.

ATTILA [RAISES HAND]: Why can't we choose
  our own? I know some good ones. Zombie
  Moonshine. Dark of the Werecats.
MRS ZIEGLER [SWIPES HAIR OUT OF EYES, SCREWS
  UP FACE——AN IMPRESSIVE SIGHT, GIVEN ALL
  HER WRINKLES]: Not a chance. I've had this
  argument nine billion times and it doesn't
  make a blind bit of difference. We have to
  follow the curriculum.
CLASS [AS ONE, ASSUMES LOOK OF MORTAL INJURY]:
  Aw.
MRS ZIEGLER [SIGHS]: Good grief. Fine. You can
  choose one——ONE!——non-list novel to analyze.
  We'll take a session to look at it at the
  end of this module. Deal? And who knows?
  [GIVES EVIL SMILE] You might end up prefer-
  ring one of these.

Uh huh.

Mrs Ziegler's a good teacher and Attila likes her, but he hates English and makes sure everyone knows. I don't mind it. At least, I don't mind writing, which is why I think I might do a book some day. (Something with astronomy—maybe a bunch of gamers get sucked into computers and end up in a different galaxy, fighting for their lives. Or maybe not exactly that—the plot seems to change every time I think about it.) Plays are okay, too.

Mrs Ziegler's all for the book idea. She says the astronomy gamers thing is a *fabulous* idea. She says to write *everything* down, and practise being *super*-accurate, and try to get the *essence* of how things make me feel (jeez), and never leave things out just because they're too uncomfortable ("the best writing comes from discomfort and pain and anger"), jeez jeez, and try different ways of doing dialogue and descriptions, and above all, *keep at it.*

I almost wish I hadn't told her, except her fussing's kind of nice. She's endearing, in a wizened way. She always has the shakes—even her hair trembles. When she gets excited, it trembles more.

Walking home from school takes Attila and me at least an hour because we're always stopping to wrangle over things. And to buy snacks, which is invariably a scrum because every other college guy has had the same idea. If you could map chocolate eating and pie scoffing, there'd be a gigantic outward-radiating wave, with its central point at school, starting at 3.15 p.m. every week day.

(I suppose you could get into the physics of it all, and map the interference patterns caused by the radiating waves of the other colleges in the city.)

(Or you could just hang a big sign saying "Nerd" around your neck and save everyone the trouble.)

Attila's real name is Patrick. He started college the same day I did, February before last, and his puns were so audaciously bad that by ten past nine he'd earned his nickname and my abiding respect. A day or so later, Attila the Pun morphed into Attila.

Coming home today we were having one of those conversations where Attila goes on about his latest obsession, and I go on about mine, and occasionally one of us notices what the other one's saying. Attila's into stand-up comedy and manga, and I'm into astronomy and web design. We're both into computer games. The more obscure the game, the better, though we're not above a fight to the death in Balldozers.

We stopped for a rest under the pohutukawa trees at the war memorial, and I piled some dried-up leaves into a red heap on the bench and mentioned that, in Chinese astronomy, Aquarius isn't Aquarius. Attila gave me the eyebrow quirk he saves for extreme stupidity, so I explained that, for the Chinese, Aquarius is part of a different constellation, The Black Tortoise of the North.

Attila got all excited and jumped on the bench and opened his arms and shouted in a thunderous voice, "Azure Dragon of the East, Vermilion Bird of the South, White Tiger of the West *aaaaand* Black Tortoise of the North!"

Maybe having that loud a voice'll be good when he's a stand-up comedian but, meantime, I moved further round the bench.

It turns out The Black Tortoise of the North and the others are characters in manga.

"I've seen some epic fights, hell yeah," Attila said. "Which reminds me. The Non-Chosen Novel. It's gotta be something sensational." He narrowed his eyes. "Something Mrs Ziegler'll have to admit's fifty times better than *Lord of the* bloody *Flies*."

I scuffed my foot on a loopy root. "*To Kill a Mockingbird*'d better have plenty of battle scenes. It's the only reason I chose it."

Apparently, people in the 1960s and 1970s thought the world was about to get a lot nicer. They said everyone would be into peace and love. There was a famous song, "Aquarius", that said peace and love would guide the stars and planets, as soon as the Moon moved into the seventh house and Jupiter aligned with Mars.

The awkward thing is, Jupiter aligns with Mars a few times every year, and the Moon's in the seventh house for a couple of hours each day, so as a predictor for a new epoch it wasn't what you could call accurate.

Also, confusingly, astrologers have wildly varying opinions about when the Age of Aquarius actually is—or will be. Depending on who's talking, we're in it now but haven't been for long, or we've been in it since 1447AD, or we won't be in it till 3597AD.

Astrology's not my thing, but it's got some good stories.

Same with mythology. For example, in ancient Egypt everyone thought the spring flood of the Nile was caused by Aquarius dipping his pitcher in the river.

I like that.

The Andromeda Galaxy
is Very, Very Big

Attila went off towards his place in Mariri Street, and I crossed the road and slogged up the steps, thinking moody thoughts about the Chosen Novel.

On the top step I paused, feeling weird. I looked around, trying to work it out, frowning at trees and houses and a prickly plant sticking through a hole in the fence.

Then I remembered.

There was no tell-tale blob of red down the street at Boyd's place, but it didn't matter. "Cowardy mouse" was back.

So. Up until a year ago, my father was famous.

Now he's a little bit infamous, and dead.

It takes a while to get used to that sort of thing. If you ever do. But I might as well admit this: the more time goes by, the more I think about the infamy.

Not that I really think about it. It belts around in my head, and if I start paying attention it shoots away, like those magnets that repel each other.

For most of my life, as I've said, my father was the illustrious Jamie Theodorus. Now he's the guy whose client died in his care. When the storm on Mount Everest passed, they found Stephen Pritcher in the snow 300 metres up from Camp Four, huddled over and lifeless. Not far, apparently, from where Dad left him and walked away.

Every now and then I like to imagine having a freakish growth spurt and ending up twice Boyd's size.

I'd stuff him up the exhaust pipe of the idiot-mobile.

Or I'd make him count the stars in the Andromeda Galaxy, on a smoggy night, through a tiny four-inch telescope.

Maybe I'll start working out with weights and turn into one of those wrestling guys with the bulging—well, everything. Whenever Boyd talks about Dad? *Bam.* Or—longer-term plan—I'll be a legendary lawyer, and sue the hell out of him if he says anything I don't like.

I could even get into climbing, and save a few mountaineers from cling-holds at the peaks of Death Zone mountains.

Except I get a bit of vertigo.

I discovered it by accident, the first time Dad took me down to the climbing wall. I think I was about six. A few times at the top I got dizzy, and after a while I figured out I wasn't that keen on near-vertical surfaces. Fen, it turned out later, was the climber— fearless, all over the wall, always niggling Dad to belay him up this course or that one. Dad was lightning fast with the clips and ropes, and his hands were sinewy and precise, and you could see everyone pretending not to watch but watching anyway.

But when it comes right down to it, you can't go around assaulting or suing or outperforming everyone who bugs you.

I might as well face it. I'll always be the guy whose father deserted a dying climber on Everest.

What makes it even worse is that Dad got so furious about other climbers making bad decisions. He always said, "When you're at the top, you're less than halfway."

Less, because getting down's harder than getting up—you're already wiped out, and your brain's so starved of oxygen you've got the mind-power of a gerbil. Most of the deaths on Everest happen on the way down.

When he was angry Dad did a thing of tilting his head and skewering you with a frown. His eyes were dark blue and seemed to burn a smoking hole in your forehead and then read your brain through it.

He didn't frown more than anyone else's dad, I guess. Maybe less than some. He laughed a lot. The skin on his face was stretched thin in some places and rumpled in others from all his time in high-altitude weather, and Mum used to wind him up by saying I didn't need to study the ancient Greeks because we already had one in the house.

"Theodorus of Crampon," she'd say. "Creator of lofty philosophies and frothy beers. And reacher for the stars. The only thing you need—" she'd pat his chin—"is a long white beard."

Then Dad would start pacing the floor in his impression of a philosopher, talking ridiculous made-up Greek.

Sometimes, out of the blue, I get a memory of him as if he's right there and not one second of the past year has happened. At those times everything's pretty much as bad as it was the first minute I heard.

Not that I'd ever tell the counsellor.

Agent Elmo

At home I made my signature dish, i.e. sludge—equal parts choc-olate powder, milk powder and sugar, mixed to a paste with milk for slurping off a spoon—and went out to the sunroom.

There's not much to see out the window, just trees, glasshouse, one red wall and the red door of the shed. When I'd licked the spoon clean I went outside and across the lawn.

I hadn't been in the shed for a long time. It was dark, crammed with crates and paint containers. The smells of linseed oil and yeast wafted around, as if Dad might be just around the corner.

Down the steps the glasshouse had the same yellow light I remembered, and the same closed-in quietness. The plants were long dead. I went out, rattling the door shut behind me.

In the hallway I was passing Fen's room when his door opened and he was standing there in his usual clothes: the red hoodie that's a year too small for him, the black tee-shirt with llamas, the less faded of his two pairs of jeans, and sneakers.

He doesn't tie his shoelaces, so wherever he goes they tick and slap along behind him. He talks like someone in a silent movie, but you can usually hear him coming.

In the gloomy hallway the smudges under his eyes looked darker, and his skin whiter. He dropped a couple of books onto the pile at the door. "All right?" I said.

He shrugged. I got a whiff from his clothes.

"Hey. Wear your other stuff tomorrow. It's clean."

He's got a second set of essentially the same things: red jersey, green tee-shirt with dragons, the more faded pair of jeans. That's it. He won't wear anything else.

He turned and half nodded, and the door closed behind him.

Luckily, his bloody-mindedness doesn't extend to underpants.

Around six I got hungry and went to find Mum.

She was in the half-dark in the spare room, asleep in the chair with a blanket hanging off her knees. A teacup was on the table with the sugar bowl and a teaspoon.

The sugar bowl is an old red thing with a chipped lid, but Mum treats it like the finest china. One time she broke it and got really upset, and it took Dad forever to fix it, night after night in the shed fiddling with the smallest pliers and the bottle of glue and hundreds of little bits. I used to go out and talk to him about black holes and quasars so he wouldn't get bored.

At least, that's what I remember thinking at the time.

Jeez.

I microwaved a couple of freezer dinners and took one, warped and steaming through its gaps, in to Fen. He was on his upper bunk in a sea of soft toys. Putting Elmo to one side, he reached for the plate.

Elmo was a present from Dad, maybe three years ago, and Fen loved him on the spot and made him Head Toy. Elmo's spot is in the top left drawer of Fen's green chest of drawers, which is kept open for him. He sits there and stares out at his furry subjects on the top bunk.

I wondered if Fen ever talked to the toys.

Then, while his fork clacked and scraped at his dinner, I leaned against the door frame and fell into a reverie where Elmo was a secret agent keeping me informed of my brother's thoughts, briefing me in urgent asides whenever Fen left the room.

Maybe, I thought, hunger was making me hallucinate. I went back for the other dinner and took it to my room.

Great Aunt Mintie

Sometimes when I'm stalling about homework and don't feel like gaming either, I fiddle around with website designs. It's strangely calming. Attila says it proves my insanity.

I'd finished dinner and was tinkering with code when I heard muffled clatters and shuffling in the kitchen. Mum's footsteps went down the hallway, and at the other end of the house a toilet flushed. Water ran into a sink, and a door opened and closed.

Things went quiet again, and the dark outside got deeper.

Later still, in the middle of a game of Balldozers, I realized the school lunches weren't likely to jump up and make themselves. I crash-shut the game and thumped down the hallway, doing a few martyred sighs along the way.

The kitchen clock said 7.45 p.m. My brain did its usual knee-jerk translation and came up with 1.30 p.m. Nepal Standard Time, and I noticed there was no bread.

Therefore no sandwiches, therefore a sprint to the corner shop before closing time at eight.

While I hunted around for my sneakers I glanced in the laundry and saw the basket overflowing across the floor, which reminded me no one had done the washing, which meant if I didn't do it now I'd be off to school in the morning without a shirt. I started hurling clothes at the machine.

My memory of Mum after the accident is of a blur of action.

She organized the memorial service, and ran it like—well, like Zeus directing his forces. She booked the counselling sessions, took us to them and stayed polite with the dozo counsellor. She talked to our teachers to get us back into the day-to-day routine of school. And she did endless inquest stuff like signing forms, going to meetings, and spending hours on the phone.

As far as I could see, she had everything covered.

Then she started making dinners and freezing them. Stacks and stacks of them. She bought a second freezer and filled that too. And she cleaned. All the time. Every room, even down to washing the curtains and shampooing the rugs.

Then she moved everything around, in every room. Then she put Dad's clothes in boxes in the attic.

Then she stopped doing anything.

Three or four of her friends started coming round. They brought lasagne and home-made bread, and hugged us all constantly.

Around then, Great Aunt Mintie arrived from Dunedin to stay in the spare room. At the airport it was weirdly great to see her crazy hair and blue eyes. Back at home and for the next few weeks, Gam and Mum sat on couches or in chairs and talked and talked, or they blocked up the hallway or random corners, talking more, or after dinner they kept talking in quiet mutters in the living room with cups of tea. Sometimes I'd hear a big roary laugh from Gam that reminded me of old times.

Great Aunt Mintie also creaked around doing shopping and washing clothes and stuff, and she made me and Fen do the vacuuming and help with the dishes.

I suppose it was what we needed. It was impossible to tell at the time because everything was standing still in a dirty fog, but looking back I guess things got calmer and steadier. Mum started buying groceries and making dinners again.

After a while Gam flew back to Dunedin, but she rang every couple of days.

I can't say if Mum was happy, exactly. That kind of thing's hard to tell. But life felt almost reasonable.

For the last three months, though, we've shot back to square one. The safest bet for finding Mum is in the green chair, where she sits looking past the curtains into the garden. Half the time she's asleep, like today. Other times you can see she's been crying. The frozen dinners have come in handy.

I'm developing a theory about it. That last week of January, just before school starts, is always crazy—renewing bus passes, shoving through bedlam at the stationery shop, poring over the mummified horrors of last year's backpacks. My theory is, that's what tipped Mum off the rails. It was our first new school year since Dad died, and (here's one thing the counsellor got right) "first time" things are hard.

The only other possible cause is Gam's funeral and the rush of flying to Dunedin for it, which was around the same time.

Mostly what I remember of that is a muddle of faces and noise. When we got home, Mum was quiet and she looked thinner and her clothes were rumpled, and she never seemed to get better. Some days she cooked dinner, but that was about it. Her friends Laura and Jessica came around less and less—she didn't ask them in, so they stood on the doorstep saying awkwardly cheerful things and then left.

It was really sad and everything about Gam, and I miss her. But in Dunedin everyone said she'd had a brilliant long life, and that her funeral should be more of a celebration than anything else, so I don't see why it should've upset Mum so much. Which is why the back-to-school thing is my number one theory.

Besides, Gam wasn't even Mum's aunt—she was Dad's.

Fen's llama-themed underpants hit the peg basket, which tipped off the dryer so the pegs scattered round the floor in a spray of green and pink plastic. I'd just put a glug of blue stuff in the machine and jabbed the buttons to start it when Mum turned up in the doorway.

I slid past her, scraping my shoulder on the door frame, and muttered, "I'm going for bread."

She watched me go past.

"For lunches," I said. "Someone's got to."

Altair & Superpowers

Outside was dark with a few wispy clouds. I slammed the gate.

What if I didn't sweat and drudge like a slave, getting all the stuff Mum forgot? Then what'd happen?

We'd starve to death, that's what.

Most of the time now, you can't see the kitchen bench under dirty dishes and blobs of food. The rest of the house is almost as bad—though once in a while, in memory of Great Aunt Mintie, I shove the vacuum around. Occasionally when the grass gets too wild I drag out the lawnmower and shove that around, too.

After the accident Mum kept up her freelance work for a while. I'd find her at the desk in their bedroom, staring at the computer screen. I don't know much about designing logos, but the process was a lot quieter than I remembered. In the old days, she'd do exercises every now and then while she worked. She'd read some-where that sitting for too long takes years off your life.

"*Years!*" she said at dinner.

"Finally," said Dad, "you realize it. The career you should have had. Mountaineering."

She gave him such a look over her glasses that Fen giggled and spat milk all over his plate.

Lately, as I've said, she's stopped doing much at all. But if I tell her she's messing up, I'll start shouting and I won't be able to stop.

Some of the trees on Upland Road look like they belong in a fairy tale. Their branches are twisted like knuckly old hands, and the trunks are hunched over with mossy stuff hanging off. Even when it's calm the leaves make a sound like far-off keyboards tapping.

Up ahead the shop owner was bent over, dragging a flap-board towards the shop. I yelled, but he disappeared into the doorway.

"Wait!" I yelled again.

He stuck his head out the door and waved. "Milk? Bread?"

"Bread." My sneakers slapped. "Toast slice. Thanks."

After the dark, the shop was bright yellow. The air in the doorway smelled like apples. "Home's Oven?" the guy called around the aisle.

"Yeah—thanks."

At the counter I rummaged in my pockets, looking vacantly at the gummy snakes in their glass jar. Luckily there was enough change in the housekeeping wallet.

Outside I crossed the road and turned for the observatory.

Up through gaps in the trees I found Altair, the brightest star in the thieving Eagle constellation (and the twelfth brightest in the night sky), but no sign of Aquarius. It's a faint constellation, as those things go.

I imagined Zeus's shepherd looking down at Earth, feeling annoyed at being stuck on Mount Olympus for all time and watching his poor old sheep wander around in a confused state.

I'm assuming he could see his sheep. Zeus would surely have

given him a superpower or two. Laser vision, at least. As a measly payback for his life of enslavement.

It's a slightly creepy walk from the end of the road to the observatory dome. There's not much light, and the plant smells are weirdly strong. Behind me the cable-car bell rang, and a second later someone whistled the same note.

A familiar shape was outside the main doors, looking up. I've known George since I was six, when I started going to the kids' astronomy club. He uses the dome for research and volunteers a few nights a month. Lately he's been letting me do my own set-ups on the telescope.

He heard me coming. "Tut. Here for viewing?"

"Nah. Out for bread."

"Just as well—it's not the best. Altair looks good, though."

The star jittered and gleamed.

George's laugh is really just a slightly audible smile. "Rotational velocity at the equator," he said, and I could hear him laughing, "Two hundred and eight-six kilometres per second."

We've always had a thing of out-nerding each other.

"Got time for a quick aloha inside?" he said. "Brett and Miriam are working up a display. Comets, if I remember."

The observatory lobby is dim with blueish lighting, and there's a quiet, almost listening feel. Miriam and Brett were out the back drinking raspberry tea and making messy notes. They're students at the university, and I've never ever seen them apart.

"Tut!" said Miriam. "Are your ears burning? Here we are talking about your namesake, and you turn up!"

Brett leaned back in his chair and mimed a high five.

We swapped a few comet facts and agreed it was lousy weather for viewing, and on the way out I called in on the Rex Johns.

The dome is up twelve steps with a varnished wooden handrail. I've been up there hundreds of times, but I still get a feeling of expectation whenever I put my foot on the bottom stair.

The first time I was allowed up there, I was a little kid and my head only reached the handrail. I peered up through the crowd, shuffling step by step, until finally I got a glimpse of the steel arches and painted timber of the high domed roof. Then the old pulleys and chains, glinting in the near dark, and the weights, and the wires snaking around the walls.

The whole thing was like magic. I remember creeping around and around, and the wooden floor creaking and shifting under the quiet scuffing of everyone's footsteps.

There was—still is—the English Regulator Clock off to one side in its case, and the glass-fronted cabinets with all the old instruments and their handwritten labels. And of course, in the middle or at least just slightly off to one side, the Rex Johns telescope.

It was made in Dublin in 1882, and the shiny black cast-iron and brass look heavy enough to flatten a house. Just being in the same room feels like genuine astronomy. The walls of the dome are white and the Rex Johns is there in the middle, gleaming and hefty-looking, and you look up through the long black slice in the ceiling and shiver in the cold and zip up your jacket and it's just thoroughly impressive.

Looking into a telescope always gives me a peculiar feeling. I stare at the brilliant dots on the black, and I get this impression of vastness and cold that makes me remember—or understand again—that everything's out there, immense and indifferent, and that I'm so insignificant I don't even begin to register on the scale of things.

I like it, in an edgy kind of way. It's alone, but not lonely. Or maybe it's lonely but in a good way.

It's hard to explain.

Dad once said solitude was what he liked about climbing.

It was in the sunroom. A few people were there drinking beer, and I was allowed to stay up. There was a slow conversation going around the room, about climbing and what makes people do it. Mike Culver, one of the climbing guides, said it was the extreme physical stuff that kept him going back—into places where he'd have to push himself to the limit.

One of the new guys nodded and said the camaraderie was amazing. "Specially on the tough trips. Pulling together, when it's hard. Facing the danger."

Dad said, "It's as close as you get to seeing the truth of things. Your own irrelevance."

Mike laughed at him and said he was going all mystical. But I knew what he meant.

The Tree of Zeus

Back home I didn't feel like going inside, so I went around the back of the house and half groped, half listened across the grass to the steps outside the living room.

My eyes got used to the dark and I picked out the pale blobs of old flowers under the trees. A cricket did a mournful scraping. I leaned out for a look at the treehouse.

It's in the biggest tree in the garden. Uncle Neal says it's an oak, and I've always liked that, because according to the ancient Greeks the oak was Zeus's tree.

Mum and Dad built the treehouse when I was eight and Fen was still a toddler.

"Don't go any higher," Dad said when it was finished. He was looping the extension cord over his arm, and he pinned me with a dark-blue stare. Mum stopped folding the workbench to add her own scowl.

Fen wasn't allowed up there for years, so I had the run of it. I did go higher a few times, feeling guilty and keeping a good eye out below, and one time I climbed far enough to discover a view right down into the city.

I also rediscovered vertigo. Luckily I made it down okay. It's a long time now since I've been up at all.

Next door, someone turned on all the garage lights and started banging around. Boyd, probably, grooming the idiot-mobile.

I wondered what Phoebe was doing.

She usually wears a long black skirt and blue shoes, and pale shirts. She has very short, very black hair, and sometimes she wears a silver choker with Zodiac charms on it. She's extremely nice to look at. I have to be careful not to stare.

I sat there a bit longer, musing, then remembered the lunches.

Twenty minutes later I was putting the butter in the fridge when I realized it was way past Fen's bedtime.

He was still on the top bunk, still surrounded by a jumble of soft toys. "Bed," I said. "Them too."

He looked mutinous for a second. But he also looked dead tired. Staying up late, I happen to know, isn't always as great as you think it's going to be.

He groaned, rolled onto his stomach and slid over the edge of the bed. I nudged his legs so they'd meet the mattress, and he monkeyed along to the ladder and down to the floor. The fluffy crab was in his fist.

While he was off cleaning his teeth, I got the animals into a pile at the foot of the bed. A seahorse and a bean-stuffed donkey ended up on top.

Fen came back and got changed behind the door, making high-pitched huffs of effort. He came out in his giraffe pyjamas, climbed onto the bunk and made a fuss, as he always does, of snarling his duvet into a big cocoon around himself. Finally he gave one last heave and a long sigh, subsided onto his pillow and looked out from inside the covers.

I pulled myself up the ladder. "So. A story."

He didn't answer.

"Just a short one," I added, which is what Dad always said.

I reached for the donkey. "A long time ago, in Greece, everyone said the sun was a god called Helios who drove around the sky in a chariot pulled by four white horses." I held up the donkey.

Fen closed his eyes.

"The chariot guy had a son called Phaethon, who kept nagging for a turn at driving. Finally, just to get a few minutes' peace, he gave in."

Fen's eyelid twitched.

"Wouldn't you know it, Phaethon was a dozo and a crap driver, and he lost control of the horses. The chariot shot up so high—" the donkey hit the ceiling and Fen's eyes snapped open— "that everyone on Earth started freezing."

Fen closed his eyes again. I said more quietly, "And then Phaethon got so scared he hurtled the chariot straight down."

Fen couldn't see my hands, I realized. I stopped waving them. "He flew the horses too close to the Earth, and scorched most of Africa into deserts."

Fen's breathing was slower.

I saw a little soft-toy man in the pile and picked it up. "Luckily, Zeus was watching. He shot Phaethon with a thunderbolt so he nosedived into a river." I ground the little man into the bed, and pounded him a few times.

Fen was asleep. I snuck out, leaving his door slightly open the way he likes it.

Xuan Wu the Dark Warrior

At lunch the next day, I told Attila about the tool-belt moment with Boyd.

'Tool belt,' he said. "Nice." He leaned back on the bench. "What'd he say?"

I pretended interest in a cloud. "Nothing much. I'm a loser. Stuff like that."

Attila pulled his feet up, stretched the full length of the bench and put his hands behind his head. "Idiot."

Then suddenly he was sitting up, slapping his feet onto the path. His lunchbox toppled and tipped out an egg-and-sardine sandwich. "We'll teach him."

I frowned.

"Humility," he expanded. "We'll teach him."

It's all right for Attila. Not everyone's built like a concrete lighthouse. "You seen his muscles lately?"

He shook his head. "We'll use stealth." He jiggled one bent leg. "Guerrilla warfare. Rocks dropped off buildings. Water bombs. He'll never know where it's coming from, but—" he squinted over the playing fields— "he'll know his karma's not working."

*

All the way home from school Attila kept up a lookout for Boyd, meanwhile adding a string of ever-gorier retributions to his list and, in between times, describing his current thoughts on the Non-Chosen Novel.

I just nodded.

At his place we made milkshakes (him: lime and caramel with yellow food dye; me: banana and almond with blue) and had a session of Torrents of Mania. Attila's attention wandered and he bombed out in the pizza round, so I crash-died in sympathy and started a fitful game of Solitaire while he went on Balldozers.

In between moves he told me about The Black Tortoise, a.k.a. XuanWu or The Dark Warrior, and how sometimes he's drawn as a human warrior with crazy black hair.

I paused the Solitaire to go looking on another site.

Maybe it was the hair, but XuanWu reminded me of Dad.

He was one of those people they call larger than life. When he wasn't on a mountain, his climbing mates came round and they'd all go in the sunroom and drink beer. Dad would tell stories and make his sudden yells of laughter, and everyone else would cluster around him like satellites.

He invented some crazy beers. It was a running joke. There was Quince and Honey Stout, Persimmon Lager and—his masterwork, he said—Tamarillo Ale. Mike Culver said it was just as well Dad wasn't as experimental with his climbing practices. "We'd be using fishing line for ropes."

In general Dad had a quick way of doing things. He got impatient with slowness. Mum sometimes sighed and said, "It's been too long between mountains. Go climb a rock," and, if he was in a

37

mood to take advice, he'd go climbing for a day. It seemed to help.

"Hey," I said to Attila. "Your Black Tortoise dude."

He grunted.

"He's right there with Beta Aquarii."

Attila does irritated incomprehension very well—the flared nostrils, the violent eyebrows, the snarly lip. He gave me the full force. "And?"

"And it's the brightest star in Aquarius."

He does scorn well, too.

The brightest star in Aquarius is about 540 light years from Earth. Which means if you could strap yourself into a rocket that belted along at light speed (and unfortunately, you couldn't, because there aren't any), it'd take 540 years to get there.

I know: impressive.

"Here," said Attila. "Gonna find the tackiest, goriest game ever made. For the hell of it."

I looked over at his screen. "It has to have a cheesy name. Like Death Rattle. Or Blood Gusher."

"Bone Cruncher Head Popper," he said.

I pulled my chair over. It's a wicker rocking chair that belonged to Attila's grandparents, and it isn't very good as a computer chair, but I've got used to stuffing the draught stopper under one runner.

"Death Star, nup … Death Race, nup … Death Grips …" Attila leaned right up to the screen. "Nup, nup, nup … Death Zone," he muttered, and his voice cut off.

When I looked I saw his face was going red. "Sorry." He pulled the computer lid down.

In a vague way I noticed everything going buzzy. "What is it?"

"Nothin'. Radio thing."

"Come on."

He pulled a face, and dragged the lid up.

Death Zone Morality, I read. *Renowned climber denounces callous mountain practices*. "Sorry," said Attila again. He closed the lid.

"It's okay," I said, and there was a silence.

Attila started talking, fast and loud. "Been thinking about the Chosen Novel. My plan's this. I'll analyze it with reference to the history of stand-up comedy."

I stared at him, but he was off.

"I'll make a whole lot of lousy comparisons. And shore 'em up with shonky facts and pointless quotes."

I said, "Wait. Aren't you doing *Lord of the Flies*?"

"I'll use three- and four-syllable words. And stuff in as many buzzwords as humanly possible. Then I'll chuck in a metaphor or two and some arty-farty opinions, and I'll be sorted." He stopped and bit the edge of his thumbnail. "That's English Crit for you," he said past his teeth. "Make things up, and make 'em sound good."

All the way home, walking in and out of dim afternoon shadows, I thought about the headline on Attila's computer and wondered if I should go find it online.

It might prepare me—what with the anniversary looming, and everything looking like being dragged up again. Or, I thought, banging through the front door, maybe I should turn a blind eye. It'd only eat away at me, making everything ten times worse.

I went looking straight away.

8,000 Metres

It was a podcast. Someone was interviewing a climber called John about high altitude climbing.

"Isn't it true," said the interviewer, "that on commercial expeditions, every client has paid between fifty and a hundred thousand US dollars for his or her chance to reach the summit?"

John agreed that yes, that was true.

"All right. Tell me what happens to the human body in the zone above eight thousand metres—the Death Zone. Where most of us would very quickly die without supplemental oxygen."

I pushed the earbuds tighter.

Some climbers say it's cheating to use bottled oxygen—you should climb without it, or not at all. I can see the point, in theory. But you wouldn't catch me up there without it.

John said, "Being at very high altitude typically causes weakness and nausea. Even above seven and a half thousand metres, most people have trouble keeping food down."

(Not that you'd catch me up there anyway.)

"Acclimatisation helps, of course. But the higher up the mountain you go, the less oxygen you're getting. There's only a third as much at the summit as there is at sea level, so you breathe three to four times faster—in and out, eighty or ninety times a minute."

"For real." The interviewer sounded impressed.

"And the effect is that, even with bottled oxygen, your brain begins to shut down."

"Exactly," said the interviewer. "I'd like to talk, now, about what people are calling Death Zone morality. Wouldn't you agree that in punishing conditions such as these, even guides sometimes can't make rational decisions about the welfare of others?"

John did not agree. "Guides need the stamina to make good decisions at altitude. And to help others. It's crucial."

"But where's the logic in rescuing some guy who's too far gone to survive?"

"How could you be sure he was too far gone?" snapped John.

They were heading into a slanging match. I closed the tab and checked if Attila was online.

Zeustian Logic: What're you doing?

AnimeTomato: homework blaagh

Zeustian Logic: Would you go past a dying climber?

AnimeTomato: ?

Zeustian Logic: If you were going up a mountain.
Like, if you'd paid $50,000 to get up Mount Everest.

AnimeTomato: hard to say.
maybe, yeah

Zeustian Logic: What??

AnimeTomato: well i mean if I'd spent that much why should i stop plus if i stopped and tried to help I'd probably die too
so yeah
what's the point of that?

Zeustian Logic: Some survive. A couple of guys got rescued once.

AnimeTomato: but they all know what they're in for

almost like it's in their contract

1 in 25 die trying right?

Zeustian Logic: Are you just saying this because of you know what?

AnimeTomato: well maybe i would if i thought it the other way but i think it this way i mean they know how insanely dangerous it is you gotta be crazy to climb that thing in the 1st place

There was a long pause.

AnimeTomato: shit

sorry didn't think that through

Zeustian Logic: Nah, it's okay.

The gate latch clinked. A few seconds later someone knocked at the front door, and a couple of bumps from the other end of the house suggested Mum was getting it.

A floorboard creaked, the doorknob rattled, some guy said about four words and suddenly Mum was yelling.

"I told you *no*! I said no! How *dare* you come back here?"

I sat upright.

She was raving, really losing it:

How could he—did he have any idea what we were going through—did he even consider? And when the guy tried to say something, Mum went quieter for about a nanosecond and then yelled, No, she wouldn't just listen, it was obscene he was here, despicable, and he'd better get off her property right now and never come back.

The door slammed so hard I jumped, knocking my arm on the chair. Mum was running down the hallway now, with wails that spread out through every room in the house.

I stayed where I was. I didn't feel altogether there. The wails carried on, every one the same.

I stood up. I didn't mean to. "Shut UP!"

I thumped down the hall, yelling louder. "SHUT UP!"

The wails stopped. She was squeezed up against the side of the bed, looking over her shoulder.

"What about Fen?" I shouted.

My voice yodelled like I was twelve.

And Mum giggled.

I was so shocked I just stared. After a bit, I left.

Out the window I saw the guy on the path, glancing back. His face was whitish in the gloom.

I *knew* his voice was familiar.

Olive out of the Bottle

I banged out the gate, already running.

Further up the street the guy leaned into the back of a silver car.

He'd turned up once before, not long after the accident, wanting to talk to Mum. It was when she was in her efficient, dinner-making phase, and she took about four seconds to tell him there was no way she'd be talking about anything, to any reporter, thanks, and she shut the door very efficiently in his face.

The guy got in the car. I was still too far away.

The engine started and the car pulled away. Then it slowed. I lunged the last few steps and banged the roof. The car stopped with a jerk, the engine cut, and the driver's door swung open. "What the *hell*?" He came at me round the end of the car.

I backed up, gabbling. "You were at our place."

He kept coming. He looked savage.

"You came to see—Rose Cornelius," I puffed. "I'm—uh—it's my dad. My dad's James Theodorus."

His face changed in an instant.

He glanced down the street and came close, and took me gently by the elbow.

"Right." He looked into my face. "Cool. That's cool. Sorry. I didn't know. Look … let's just have a quick chat here, right? Whaddya think, yeah?"

I shrugged, and wondered what I was doing, exactly.

"Just you and me." He took his hand off my elbow and patted my shoulder.

I felt panicky. "I just wanted—"

What did I want? After a second of frowning at Mrs Jarvis's white picket fence, I got it.

Maybe Mum couldn't be bothered defending Dad. But I could.

She'd sent every reporter away—not just this guy. There were plenty, especially at first, but she always sent them off.

"I just wanted to say—" I said, and stopped again.

The guy did about ten rapid nods. "Sure. Sure. Whatever you want. Take your time. I'll just—" He leaned in the passenger door and shoved over to the back seat, reaching. "Y'mind?" he said in a muffled voice, and unwound himself from the car. He was holding a little black gadget. "Just get the facts straight. Keep a record is all. Wouldn't want to mess up, right?"

"Um, oh, actually—no," I said. "Sorry. I don't want—"

He came two quick steps closer. "No, no, it's all good. Absolutely." He nudged me, shoulder to shoulder. "You just take your time, no pressure. Just if you want to say anything, you know—" he glanced towards our place— "set the record straight—" He polished the voice recorder with the side of his thumb. "Must've been hard. Must've been awful, I'd think. Hearing all that … stuff. About your dad."

He bent over the recorder, jabbed a button, and looked up. "Must've hurt. Specially if it wasn't true. Huh? Never happened the way they said?"

I took a couple of steps back. I was thinking it was a mistake, the whole thing.

"They said some shitty things, yeah?"

I didn't answer.

He shook his head. "Like they'd know." The recorder winked a red light. "Like they'd know what it's like—up there." He rolled his eyes upward, like Mount Everest was just above us. "Everyone's an expert. About—what is it—yeah, the Death Zone. All that." He came closer and peered in my face. "Am I right?"

I shrugged.

"Online forums," he snorted. "Everyone's got their bit to say. As if—like any of them's been in a hundred miles of the Death Zone, right? Like they've got the least idea. Turkeys."

Maybe talking to Attila had got me started. The first olive out of the bottle. "I just didn't …" I said.

And without meaning to, I started telling him.

"He wasn't like that," I said. And, "I don't think he'd have done it." And also, "He'd never just *leave* someone. He just—"

The reporter kept nodding, tilting his head and frowning, occasionally giving little clicks of his tongue.

I stopped.

The guy looked down the street again. "So, ah. Duncan. How's the family, ah … coping, would you say?"

I didn't answer.

He waited a second. "Your mum. How's she doing?"

I didn't answer.

"She seems kind of … well." He shrugged. "Understandable, of course. Course it is."

"I'm not talking about them. You just—everyone—you all think he'd do that. But," I stopped again. "He wouldn't."

There was silence, except for a bus droning up a far-off hill.

"Right. Right," said the guy. "And uh, what about young—" he leaned on the car, tapped the roof and frowned— "Fergus, is it? No—Fenton. How's he doing? Poor little guy. It's the young ones. Find it hard. Specially if the mum's not—you know, maybe not ... quite managing." He scratched his head with the voice recorder. "Not the way the little fella might need."

There was another silence.

"That's none of your business," I said. In the second of quiet I'd gotten furious.

"Hey, whoa—hold on, mate." He held up his hands. "Hold on there. Just trying to help. If mum's not coping—I mean, just say ... she feeding you enough? Keeping you clean? Warm?" He cast a thoughtful eye down my clothes. "You look a bit ... *thin*."

The fizzing in my ears almost blotted out what he was saying.

"You can piss right off." Something felt dangerous, distracting me, but I kept going. "Family stuff's our business. It's our business if she's not coping." The dangerous thing popped up again, and I yelled over it. "Or if Fen's not." I backed away, jabbing a finger at him. "I can look after him."

I turned and took off down the street. It felt like the sky was falling.

Mystic Parka

I kicked the treehouse wall and thought up a few dozen expletives for the reporter. Then I thought up a lot more, for me.

The guy would go straight to his office and write a long article, about how the son of James Theodorus whined that his father wouldn't have done what everyone says he did.

And everyone would read it and think, What a loser.

I'd have to tell Mum.

Or … I could hope nothing came of it.

Had I really said that much about Dad? Was there anything the guy could actually use?

Instead of details, the fizzing came back.

Anyway—besides—I'd told him he couldn't record me.

I really didn't feel like telling Mum. I kept thinking back, unwillingly, to her wailing.

A streamlined tui shot through a gap in the leaves, opened its wings like parachutes and landed with a flurry on a lower branch.

I'd risk it. With any luck, the guy would get distracted by a bigger story.

Then I remembered Fen.

He was in the darkest corner of his lower bunk, up against the wall with his face pushed into his knees. I ducked under the top bunk and shuffled in next to him. Everything was quiet—just the tui jabbering outside and Fen's snuffling breath.

"She's okay," I said.

He shook his head, and muttered something into his knees.

"She lost it, is all. That guy wanted to bring everything up again, and she got upset."

He wasn't having it. He pulled his shoulders up around his ears and hunched further into himself.

"It's nothing to worry about. Really."

He whispered, "She sounded like she was *dying*."

"I know." I leaned against him. "It'll be okay."

Personally, I wasn't sure. For about two seconds Mum's giggle had made me furious, but from then on I was scared. Pictures bobbed in my head of her in a green robe, screaming and running down hospital corridors.

A book was lying on Fen's pillow. I nudged it to turn the spine to the light. "Hey. One of the all-time best books."

He didn't move.

"When Archimedes goes, 'There is no boy'? Best bit. No contest."

He looked up. His face was stripy wet and dry.

"She's really okay?"

I nodded, mentally crossing fingers. "You can depend on it."

He frowned slowly around the room, then out the window. And sighed, almost absentmindedly. We sat for a while listening to the tui. There's something about those birds. When I die (at a good ripe age, maybe ninety-eight?), I want tui song at my funeral.

I wished Fen would say something.

I started manoeuvring out from between the bunks. "I'll get chocolate milk. Stay where you are."

I was almost across the room when he said, "It's not the best bit." He was pointing at *The Sword in the Stone*. "It's when they get turned into fish. In the moat."

Well. I wasn't going to argue.

Ever since Fen was about three, we've had this thing that chocolate milk gives us superpowers. When I handed it over, with a bowl of cereal in case he was extra hungry, I said, "What is it this time?"

He balanced the tray on his straightened-out legs and said, "Stretchy, I guess," but he wasn't that interested. He poked around in the bowl for a yoghurt-covered raisin and put it in his mouth.

I left him looking calmer, surrounded by messy paper and pens and drawing something from his book. The second I closed his door, I got a craving for hot chocolate. Sometimes a sludge isn't enough. Sometimes you need the luxury of hot frothed-up milk. I went to the kitchen, keeping a wary eye out for Mum, but there was no sign of her. It suited me.

When I got back to my room Attila was online.

AnimeTomato: so—
anagrams, eh?
i'm mystic parka.
gonna change my username

I had no idea what he was talking about.

AnimeTomato: except i can't decide.
which is better?—mystic parka? or karmic pasty?

He goes off the deep end sometimes.

AnimeTomato: or arty imp sack?
anagrams—geddit? mix the letters round, get new words
SO: patrick ayms = mystic parka.
and the best of the lot—
yacks armpit.

Glasspack Mufflers
& Hotdog-style Resonators

In English the next day, Attila brought up the Non-Chosen
Novel.

MRS ZIEGLER [BANGS THROUGH DOOR, STOOPED,
    SQUINTING & RUMMAGING IN HER GREEN LEATHER
    SATCHEL]: All right. The plot so far in your
    chosen novel. At least a page. Go.
CLASS BURSTS INTO DISCORDANT ACTIVITY.
MRS ZIEGLER [BAWLING OVER NOISE, STILL
    RUMMAGING]: And it's not too early to keep
    your eyes peeled for themes. [SCRATCHES HAIR
    WITH FREE HAND] Motifs. Symbols.
ATTILA [OVER NOISE]: I've got suggestions for
    the Non-Chosen Novel.
MRS ZIEGLER [LOOKS UP FROM SATCHEL WHILE
    FUMBLING GLASSES ONTO FACE AND FROWNING]:
    Is that Patrick?
ATTILA: We should decide on it now. Then we

can figure out themes and stuff at the same
time as we do them for our boring books.
CLASS MURMURS.
MRS ZIEGLER [ATTEMPTS TO HIDE SMILE]: Give
them an inch, right? [DROPS SATCHEL ON FLOOR
BESIDE HER DESK] You'll have to decide
on the non-curriculum novel amongst
yourselves—
ATTILA [INTERRUPTS]: Exactly. I did a
spreadsheet over the weekend—
MRS ZIEGLER [INTERRUPTS]: In your own time.
There's no way you're cluttering up my
classroom with a debate on the relative
merits of Pulp 1 and Pulp 2. [POINTS A
CROOKED FINGER AT ATTILA] Plot, you hellion.
Now.
ATTILA: Fine.
MRS ZIEGLER [SEVERAL MINUTES LATER, SIGHS]:
If you must, you may put your spreadsheet on
the pinboard. At the end of the period.

She came over later and asked how my story was going. She said
it's *super* I'm still doing some writing, and that it doesn't matter
what, and that it's crucial to write even if you don't feel like it, and
that it's very much like training for a marathon, in that you have
to do some *every day*.

Then she went off on a bit of a tangent, scratching her hair and
looking horrified, about how she's never been in a marathon and
never will, so it's not the ideal analogy. Then she drifted off to the
whiteboard and scrawled a thing about motifs.

53

Walking home, Attila kicked stuff along under the trees on Abel Smith Street and went into a monologue about his Non-Chosen Novel spreadsheet—who'd filled in what, who he'd managed to wheedle into choosing the best one, who'd suggested other (laughable) possibilities, and on and on.

I didn't feel like joining in, but he didn't notice.

"... *Sheep Trolls* is running close, but it's gonna be *Vampironimo*." He smacked a fist into his other palm. "And it sure as hell—" He glanced behind, and stopped.

I turned.

Boyd's car was at the lights on the expressway, first in its lane.

The car revved, surged forward, then rocked as the brakes hit. It roared again, jolted forward and braked. Boyd grinned out the driver's window at the car next to him. The other driver was looking away, down Willis Street.

A faint beat came across the traffic, and inside the car Derek nodded in time. Even at that distance he looked intense. The engine revved into a howl.

I turned. "Let's go."

Behind us, cars accelerated with a rush of noise.

We trudged up the street towards the university. Someone's purple letterbox had a newspaper poking out of it, which instantly reminded me of the reporter.

I'd been thinking about him all day, off and on. In my head he was hunched over a desk with the voice recorder, listening on headphones and typing at a keyboard. Every now and then he'd grin evilly out his window. Then he'd go back to typing.

I didn't feel like gaming, so Attila headed for his place and I went home. At our letterbox I grabbed the newspaper, pushed through the gate, sat on a rock and scoured every page.

No trumpeting headlines. I looked up, feeling dizzy but suddenly cheerful, and kicked the gate shut.

Next door, Boyd and Derek started up the idiot-mobile.

Judging by the shouting and guffawing, they were thrilled about something. Boyd started scream-revving the car so it belched out blue smoke, which meant they had to shout even louder over the noise, and in the twenty seconds or so before I could grab my bag, shovel up the newspaper, get inside and slam the door, I learnt more than I ever want to know about glasspack mufflers and hotdog-style resonators.

I'd just slung my bag into the corner of my room when someone tapped on the door and it swung open.

It was Mum. I think my jaw might have dropped.

She didn't say, "Good day at school?" Or even, "Like a bite to eat?" She said, "I'm sorry."

I stood there like a dozo until I thought to ask, "What for?'

"Shouting at the reporter. Scaring you."

She was looking around the room. I had a feeling she might start in at me to clean it up, like in the old days. Instead she said, "When Mintie died, it hit me. It was much harder than I would've expected. It was almost like …"

She stopped talking. Eventually I shuffled.

"Almost like losing Jamie again," she finished.

"What?"

A second later, I sort of got it. Great Aunt Mintie was so like Dad. Her crazy hair. Her laugh. Her presence.

Though really, it didn't make that much sense. I needed to think about it.

"Anyway," she said. "Well, anyway. I just wanted to say."

She backed out, closing the door.

The Fellowship

Mum's long silences, and the sentences that weren't actual sentences, shot me straight back almost a year to when it all happened.

It was early morning, maybe six, and Mum woke me up from a dream about the observatory. In fact, she turned up in the dream, standing at the top of the steps of the Rex Johns room, calling me. Then I woke up and realized she was by my bed.

She said she was sorry, but I had to get up. I thought it sounded like she'd been crying, and I got up on my elbows to see, but she was just a dark shape.

She went to wake Fen, and I groped around for my jersey and followed the light down to the kitchen.

I could hear Mum muttering, and Fen's higher-pitched voice. In a minute he shuffled into the kitchen, looking pale, with Mum behind him. His hair stuck up in a sheaf. Mum's cheeks were wet, with hair stuck to them. My throat hurt.

Mum pulled out chairs at the table for Fen and me, and sat in another one. The phone was in front of her. Her eyes kept sliding off to the clock on the wall. She said again how sorry she was, and crossed her hands in front of her.

The silence seemed to thump.

"Dad," I said.

She started talking like she'd been waiting for a stage prompt.

"There's a storm on the mountain. No one knows exactly what's happened. But people are missing. They think ten."

Air was pressing on my ears, and a quiet corner of my brain wondered what the hissing noise was.

Mum went on. "Dad—Dad's missing."

Fen turned to me, then to Mum. "They're looking for him?"

"It's night. It's a blizzard. The ones that got down to Camp Four, they're in bad shape. A couple are in radio contact with Base Camp. Off and on."

"But—that's good, isn't it?" said Fen.

She looked over. "Maybe, love."

I was surprised to hear my own voice. "Oxygen?"

Mum angled towards me like she could stop Fen from hearing. "It's hours since anyone's seen the others. And it's twenty-four hours since they started out. The conditions are so bad." Her voice missed so the last part of "bad" was a whisper, but it came back. "He would have run out hours ago. The longer they stay in the … the longer they're up there, the less likely…"

The longer they stay in the Death Zone, I thought.

"What?" Fen said in a half-yelp, half-wail. "Why are you crying?"

"Love," said Mum, and pulled Fen's hand towards her. "Of course we'll keep hoping. We are still hoping. But—" She sniffed, and gulped. "Without oxygen and proper shelter … I'm afraid—it doesn't look good."

Fen screamed like a shot animal, and hurtled back in his chair. It tipped and he crashed out of the room.

After a few seconds Mum said, "I need to … It's Fen. Are you—?"

I nodded and she went.

I felt blurred and far away. Thoughts wisped through. My father had died in a storm on Everest while I was warm and dry in bed. The two things couldn't happen at the same time.

Occasionally I remembered I was in the chair at the table, and I wondered if time had passed, and if so how much. It seemed like hours, or maybe a few minutes. Then I'd drift off again.

I heard Fen's voice go up in a scream and drop away, then climb again in panicky sobs. Mum's voice was there too, droning and muttering. He started a frantic whining and Mum's voice got louder, "I know, love," then died down again to a murmur.

It's not great, bringing it all up again.

Zeustian Logic: Hey.
Mystic Parka: yesss
Zeustian Logic: You started the algebra?
Mystic Parka: well now
i am following a higher calling.
—mining Anagram GOLD.
Zeustian Logic: ?
Mystic Parka: example: your friend BOYD LARSEN.
sample anagram: BONER SADLY.
Zeustian Logic: Huh. Not bad.
Mystic Parka: not BAD??
hell yes! !
also: Bra Done Sly.
And …
Randy Lobes.

Zeustian Logic: Reaching.

Mystic Parka: Bandy Loser. Dry Lone Abs. Randey Slob.

Zeustian Logic: You can't spell.

Mystic Parka: i am at the dawning of a journey of discovery

Zeustian Logic: So. You started the algebra?

I started the algebra.

I kept thinking about Mum's apology, and her silences. And about Great Aunt Mintie. I grabbed the laser pointer and made scribbly snarls on the walls, then went onto the observatory site. Someone had just posted.

Weather permitting, the next two to three nights will see a spectacular display courtesy of Jupiter and a beautiful crescent moon.

The delicate lunar sliver will appear very close to Jupiter. In fact, for a time it will seem to lie directly above the mighty planet!

So. A good viewing night. I glanced into the corner, pondering.

According to my parents, and I guess I believe them, Tuttle was my first word.

I was in the baby bouncer in the living-room doorway, and they were in the kitchen, and I started jumping up and down and yelling, pointing at the TV. They thought I was saying "turtle" but when they looked they saw the program was about Comet Swift-Tuttle.

I can't remember not being crazy about comets, stars, planets, moons, asteroids, so I suppose it makes sense.

About two-and-a-half years ago, Mum and Dad bought a baby-sized telescope second-hand from a guy at the observatory, and gave it to me—"to the family, really, but if you're very careful you can be in charge," Mum said—for my twelfth birthday. When it's not outside pointing at the sky, the telescope sits in the corner of my room. It's a reflector type, Dobsonian mount, with an optical diameter of 114mm and a focal length of 900mm. The focal ratio is f/7.9.

Not that you really needed to know all that, maybe.

Mystic Parka: hey. you there?
Zeustian Logic: What?
Mystic Parka: Boyd Larsen Toolboy
score!
gives you: Baboon Rooted Slyly.
YES? /
i mean
and hey—Leotards-Only Booby.
N O T   B A D??!
or . . . Royally Toned Boobs.
eh? come on. gotta admit.

The night of my birthday it took forever to get dark.

We assembled the telescope in the sunroom. Dad got kind of intense about it, frowning over the page and griping about opaque instructions, and Mum said he was taking over, but I didn't mind.

Fen started chucking bits of packing stuff around, so Mum took him away and it was just me and Dad. I remember carefully screwing things together, Dad muttering calculations and softly swearing, me going to the window every couple of minutes to check the sky. By chance, that week Jupiter was the closest it would get to Earth all year—and in the best place for viewing. I couldn't wait to see it.

We went outside before it was really dark, but by the time we'd got the scope into the darkest corner and sitting right, Jupiter was up and already looking amazing. Mum and Fen came out to see.

All four of the Galilean moons, i.e. the ones Galileo discovered, were there. Io was orange. It was a calm night, and finally really dark, and we stood in the cold air taking turns to look through the scope. I felt all mature, which makes me cringe now because I was still such a baby, and from what I remember I blabbered moronically about the composition of the moons.

Zeustian Logic: You still there?
Mystic Parka: yuh
Zeustian Logic: Reporters have to be fast, right?
Doing reports?
News etc.?
Mystic Parka: sure
oh yeah
from what i hear they get like an hour. start to finish.
Zeustian Logic: Yeah. Thought so.
Mystic Parka: gotta be good under pressure.
demented deadlines.
wait
what
you thinking like a CAREER? ?
Zeustian Logic: Nah. Just wondering.
Mystic Parka: wait
WAIT WAIT

HOW did I miss this? *how*?
just got a jawstomping idea

I shuffled, sculpting a better seat in the bean bag, and sighed.

Zeustian Logic: Yeah, what?
Mystic Parka: non-chosen novel.
Zeustian Logic: Well?
Mystic Parka: gonna write it myself

Ten minutes later he was back.

Mystic Parka: bang.
got it.
story sorted. start to finish.
plot. tension. all the crap Mrs Z dies for.
characters even.
And ... —the title, you ask?
<< Fellowship of the Soulless FangMen >>
brain-blowing?
or what?

Someone in Blue

A couple of days after we heard the news, Mum and Uncle Neal went to Nepal, and Mum's friend Laura came to stay with me and Fen. I don't remember much except the food was different.

A couple of weeks later on a sunny morning, Mum came home. She was quiet, but so was everyone else.

Uncle Neal stayed for a cup of tea. Then he hugged everyone and left. Soon after that, Laura left too.

So it was just the three of us. I drifted around the house, taking sneaky glances at the other two, wondering what they were thinking. I didn't seem to be thinking anything at all. Fen moped around, but always near Mum—hovering or glancing up or listening for her. Later he went into hibernation, but for those first few weeks he was always close.

The next day Mike came over.

His hair is light brown and it was cut short, and he's not like Dad at all, but standing there at the door with his wind tan and the wrinkles on his face, plus the windbreaker and his messed-up climber hands and the old carabiners hanging off his belt, he looked a lot like him. I got an intense memory of the climbing meetings in the sunroom. I could almost smell beer.

After a while Mike gave a gentle push on my arm and went past, and Mum came down the hallway, and everyone went into the kitchen and sat around the table.

It was a lot like when Mum told us about Dad, except that this time it was daytime. And Mike was doing the talking.

He didn't seem to know how to start. He put his elbows on the table, ducked his head and swiped his hands a few times across his stubbly hair.

"It was a freak storm," he said.

His freckles looked bigger, and darker. "Something they didn't predict. No one's fault. Everyone was unwell. With the ice. And wind. It was … a hell of a storm." He rubbed his face. "Very hard. For people to help each other."

That was when Mum got up and started for the door.

Fen popped up like toast, but Mike said in a louder voice, "That's all right, bud. Rose's okay. She's going for a rest, we'll give her some space, eh?"

Fen looked at Mike, then at Mum. She was at the door already.

"She'll be fine in a bit," said Mike.

Mum went out. For about three seconds we listened to her walk down the hallway. Then Fen bolted for the door.

Mike jumped up and got him in a big hug. "I want to go with her," Fen kept yelling, but Mike just mumbled about it being all right, she'll be fine, just hold in there, buddy. It took a while, but finally he eased Fen back into the chair.

Then he told us, slowly and carefully, that nine people had died.

"They couldn't help each other. They were too unwell. And there was almost no visibility."

They'd found six of the climbers, he said. Three were still missing. Including Dad.

Fen made another shot for the door. Mike grabbed for him, but gave up. "Okay. Off you go."

I got up to go too.

"Wait, Tut. You'll have to hear this soon enough." He gestured for me to sit, and I did. "I'm afraid it's not as simple as we told Fen. We have to tell him ... an easier story."

I didn't like this.

Mike looked gloomy. "There's things in the papers."

I shook my head.

He nodded. "I'm sorry. It looks like—ah, hell."

I don't remember much, mostly his frown.

"Y'see," he said. "It looks like Jamie ... I'm afraid ..." He said it in a rush. "It looks like he left one of the clients. He stopped on the way down, but ... he didn't help. He went on."

I could see one end of the rope tattoo on Mike's arm.

"We wouldn't have told you. If we could've somehow ... but we knew you'd see it. No way around it."

And then Mum turned up, magically, almost like she'd been hanging around in the hallway, and gave me a smothering hug over the back of the chair. "Fen," she muttered over my head at Mike. "Sunroom. Seems calmer."

Mike was watching me. "You all right?"

I shrugged.

Mum bent over me again. I leaned away. "I'm fine."

"Come through, love. The sunroom."

I wouldn't. They tried a while longer, then went through to the other room. I could hear murmuring but no recognizable words. I went and sat on the front doorstep.

65

It was still sunny.

After a while Mike came out. He passed me and turned, half reaching to shake my hand, then changed his mind.

"Try to take it easy," he said.

I didn't answer.

He crunched away down the path. Out of the corner of my eye I watched him go. His windbreaker swished past the shrubs.

When the gate latch clinked I got up and ran after him. With the gate between us I blabbed, "How do they know? How do they know he did it?"

He pulled at the sleeves of his jacket. "Tuttle. It was bloody confused up there. Unbelievably wild. But—this is the thing. Someone wearing blue … left someone else."

I took that in. Dad's gear was blue.

"One of our party saw it happen," said Mike. "From lower down. He saw Stephen, the client, raise his arm. He saw them talk." He snorted. "As much as you could talk—blasting ice, you could barely stand. And then the guy in blue went down. Past Stephen.

"The other climber," Mike went on. "He couldn't help. He got himself to the tents, but after that …Tut. There's only a couple of guys it could've been. Only a couple wearing blue. And the climber thought it was your dad."

Nothing moved in the garden. "The … man," I said. Maybe, I was starting to think, I could talk to him.

Mike pulled his jacket tighter. "Died. In the tents." Then he sort of patted my shoulder and went off down the street.

Of course, after that I went straight online. And there it all was.

Giant Jupiter &
Sirius the Dog Star

Around eight I got Fen settled with a story, which he barely acknowledged.

Finally it was dark enough for viewing.

Sirius, the dog star, sparkled and bustled like a gnat on fire, but Jupiter was calm and still.

The cold was making me clumsy, but finally the telescope was ready. It was a good night for viewing: dark and clear, with almost no clouds.

Next door's front door opened and closed.

It was Phoebe. I stood up taller and shuffled, hoping she'd glance over, but she didn't. She walked off down the driveway, head down and hands shoved into her pockets.

I waited around for a while, thinking she might have gone to the corner shop and that maybe I'd say something smooth when she came back. But she didn't come back, and I gave up.

Nothing smooth had come to mind, anyway.

Sirius is the alpha star of Canis Major, the Great Dog constellation.

Voyager 2, the space probe launched by NASA in 1977, is heading off in the direction of Canis Major. Unfortunately, it's like Pioneer 11—when it gets there in a few thousand years, its batteries will be well and truly fried. It won't be able to report all the exciting stuff it finds. Imagine being a rocket scientist on the team and knowing that.

At the exact instant I edged the telescope into position to pick up Jupiter, a familiar whang came from next door. The garage door crashed open, and a glaring sweep of light left me blinded and blinking. And enraged.

There was no point staying.

Dismantling the telescope went a lot faster than setting it up. I was bumping through the dark house, mentally listing the day's crappy highlights, when I saw light under the sunroom door and found Fen in the captain's chair, wrapped in his duvet and looking little and miserable in the light from the lamp. His hair was stuck down with sweat on one side.

"What—?" I lowered the telescope onto the rug. "It's late."

He mumbled something that included "nightmare" and "constellations" and straight away I knew what had set him off.

It was an old book about the Zodiac, filled with paintings of scorpions and lions, with serpent tails twisting through everything. I'd seen it in the library and thought he'd like the pictures.

"Right," I said. "You're coming with me. Observatory."

He did a gobby-mouthed frown.

"Remember the chimpanzee nightmares? Mum took you to the zoo to see real chimpanzees, and it stopped the dreams?"

He looked dubious.

"So," I said. "Observatory."

He didn't argue. I guess going outside in the middle of the night trumps most things.

On the way there he stayed close, especially on the darker parts of the observatory path. Once we were inside he was a lot happier. The glittering brass of the Rex Johns telescope grabbed him like a magnet—he was almost cheerful.

George told us he was about to head down for a coffee break. He waved a hand at the telescope. "Have a turn. You do the set-up." His footsteps tromped down the stairs and his voice floated back. "You practically live here, anyway."

I didn't let it show, but I felt pretty good about that.

First, I took Fen to see the constellation chart.

Judging by his face it was nothing like he expected, and it's no surprise—it's just a bunch of spiky lines and dots. Pretty much the opposite of the pictures in his library book, with their fangs and scaly tails. I can see why astronomers go for the simple option—you can't have Leo's mane, say, flopping all over galaxies and black holes—but I could also understand Fen's confusion.

I got the feeling the view in the telescope was a let-down too. I don't know what he expected. Surely he didn't think there'd be bears and lions up there?

I showed him Rigel and Betelgeuse in the Orion constellation, which are the sixth and eighth brightest stars in the night sky, and gave him a watered-down version of the myth of Orion and Scorpius, which is where the hunter Orion got too full of himself and Mother Earth sent a huge scorpion to fight him, and they had an epic battle until Scorpius slaughtered Orion.

I could just about see the story walking across Fen's face. He was like a little pale version of Mum, big-eyed and serious. But he swore he was fine. No more nightmares, he said.

George was back by then. He did his noiseless laugh and said, "Betelgeuse. Approximately six hundred and forty-three light years distant from Earth."

On the way home, particularly once we were back under street lights, Fen got almost talkative. He wanted to chatter about all the stuff he'd seen in the gift shop: the dinosaur puzzles, the mugs with goofy aliens, the astronaut badges. The spaceship chocolates, in particular.

I was more interested in the new poster about exploding stars.

"There's a star in the Carina constellation headed for kablooey. All set to self-destruct, any day now, in a spectacularly violent explosion. Mind you," I added quickly, "any day now in astronomy-speak means between now and a million years from now."

He wasn't worried. "Where's the crab?"

Ah. His fluffy crab. I looked up, but clouds had started drifting over. "It's not far from Orion."

We walked a bit further. "The second brightest star in the Crab constellation is Asellus Australis," I said. "Also known as the Southern Donkey Colt."

He looked surprised.

"It also enjoys the name—" I slowed down— "Arkushananga-rushashutu."

He actually giggled. I felt ridiculously pleased.

We were almost at the corner of Glasgow Street and Upland Road when I heard the shriek of a revved-up engine, getting louder fast. A second later an airhorn went off.

A car jigged around the corner from the shops, accelerating towards us. In the dark the headlights were like skewers. The engine howled.

70

We were lit up like tenpins.

The driver started engine-braking, screaming down through the gears, and the car crossed the middle line. It came straight at us, its engine still revving insanely.

I looked down at Fen. His hands were over his ears and he was pushing against me. I turned back to the lights and shouted, and put my middle fingers in the air and shoved them up and down.

The car's brakes gripped. Its nose dipped and the engine noise dropped away.

I pushed Fen towards the trees. "Go. Get out!"

He stumbled and stopped. His eyelashes flicked, black in the white light. For that second everything was still—the car crooked in the middle of the road, the engine sighing and sputtering. Hot metal tinked.

Two guys swooped out the doors and came for us.

"Go!" I yelled again.

Someone shouted, just a grunty noise, and with a crunch of gravel Fen took off. I went after him into the dark.

Two sets of footsteps pounded after us, catching up.

Fen yelped something. He was slowing down. I got his wrist and pulled him with me, yelling at him to keep going. The guys were so close I heard a shoe squeaking every time it hit the path, and the click of someone's zip tag.

Behind us came a scuffle and a crazy shout, then a long thud and a whoosh of air shooting out of lungs. Tree root, I thought. Wild swearing followed us, but no footsteps. We kept running.

Four or five corners later, I slowed and stopped and bent over to breathe. Fen skittered to a standstill. His breathing was high-pitched and quick.

After a few seconds I muttered, "Let's go."

71

All the way home, with Fen scurrying to keep up, I kept seeing the car driving at us, and hearing the blare of the horn, and feeling Fen pushing into my side. I ran through a hundred plans. Tacks on the road. Stones hurled from trees. Glue in the locks. I invented excruciating, limb-ripping fates for boy racers everywhere.

But in particular, for Boyd and his great mate Derek.

The Chimpanzee Effect

I thought Fen would be a wreck. We'd be back to square one. But, no—he was peculiarly cheerful.

I wondered what the grief counsellor would think. He'd probably get Fen to write a letter.

Maybe it's the chimpanzee effect. Maybe being part of the real thing makes it less scary. As he changed for bed, Fen kept poking his head around the door and saying, "What about when …"

He talked while he brushed his teeth, which got messy.

Twenty minutes later he was blinking out from his duvet cocoon. I said goodnight, turned off the light, closed his door—then opened it again when he squeaked indignantly—and went to my room.

Karmic Pasty: FINALLY.

where the hell you been?

Zeustian Logic: Jeez. Karmic Pasty now?

Karmic Pasty: never mind that.

—hit a snag.

Zeustian Logic: Yeah, what?

Karmic Pasty: non-chosen novel

—Soulless FangMen.

got 1000 words

and i worked something out—

they need an everyday name and an OtherOrb name.

Zeustian Logic: OtherOrb. Nice.

Karmic Pasty: you have NO IDEA.

and (ready for the genius touch?)—

the OtherOrb name IS AN ANAGRAM OF the everyday name.

Zeustian Logic: Right.

Karmic Pasty: yep.

& here's the thing

Yellowcur's one of the leaders, right?

and in the OtherOrb he's pure evil.

well. his anagram's Cruel Yowl.

red hot, yes?

Zeustian Logic: Not bad. What's the snag?

Karmic Pasty: yeah.

the main guy.

his name's Grey Brigand & his anagrams are crap.

best i can get—Drab Gingery.

Beggary Rind.

I tried, but I couldn't stay focused on the FangMen.

Who drives a car straight at a seven-year-old? Maybe I should tell someone. The police, or something.

Karmic Pasty: Slantfang Red?

best = Strangled Fan.

& this is no better: Grandest Flan.

then there's Patchfur One-Eye.

= Feathery Pounce.

I kid you not.

Of course, if I squealed, Boyd would just find a way to get revenge.

Karmic Pasty: hey—you there?

Zeustian Logic: Yeah.

Karmic Pasty: BELIEVE me.

Patchfur is *a killing machine*.

it literally couldn't be worse.

Zeustian Logic: So maybe don't do anagrams?

Karmic Pasty: nah.

rather change their everyday names, gimme half an hour.

The Beaufort Scale

The next morning Attila started talking before I was even in earshot. I caught scraps about Slantfang Red and Yellowcur, or maybe Patchfur.

Fen went off to Mrs Conrad at the corner, and Attila fell in beside me and started up again. I talked over him. "Boyd drove the idiot-mobile at me and Fen."

He stopped mid-word.

"Revving like hell. Airhorn going. The lot."

Ahead, Fen and Mrs Conrad turned the corner. Attila was open-mouthed. "Scared the crap out of Fen," I said.

Saying it made me feel kind of worse and kind of better. It brought back the rage, but it was good to tell someone.

I didn't mean to say the rest. It came out anyway.

"He says I'm a coward like Dad."

I suppose it had been sitting there, waiting to be said.

Of course, Attila was all set to go round to Boyd's place and demand an apology for driving at me and Fen. I've noticed it before—he doesn't have a WARNING! WARNING! light in his head to stop him doing insane things. Which is another reason why, walking home from the sports centre after school, I wasn't surprised when he started in.

We'd passed the wind sculptures and, as always, argued about what number they indicated on the Beaufort Scale. Attila thought a six, me a five. Then he said, "Why's it bug you so much? Your dad going past the guy on the mountain?"

At first I thought I wouldn't answer. I'd stay quiet and he'd get the message. But he kept on walking, watching his feet, and it was obvious he was getting keyed up. Finally I thought, Stuff it.

"I don't think he'd have done it," I said.

A couple of trucks boomed past, engine-braking for the lights. Attila kept plodding, not saying anything, but every now and then scratching his cheek. I didn't tell him what bugs me most. Which is that I think I feel worse about Dad supposedly leaving that dying guy than I do about the other people who died.

How sick is that?

Attila started waving his arms, and said it all came down to logic. "He couldn't help the other guy. So it'd be illogical to try and save him. Because then he'd die with him, right? It wouldn't make sense."

There was no warning, I felt rage bulging around my eyes and a pressure in my ears and I started yelling, saying it wasn't about logic, but even as I was saying it I knew I couldn't tell him what the hell it was about.

Attila looked kind of flabbergasted, and we left it.

I tried to think. Who in their right mind cracks up like that? Other than a little kid, that is. Was I going crazy?

Maybe all the stewing about the reporter was getting to me. I was still waking up at night sweating, picturing front-page headlines. And Mum reading them. But Attila must be right. The deadline must have passed.

I had to get a grip.

I kicked a stone through the fence and past a seagull, which flapped off the last bleacher onto the playing field. "Sorry," I muttered. Then, since I was on a roll, I said it to Attila too.

He frowned. "What for?"

"Aw—y'know.'"

He looked blank. I sighed. "Freaking out."

"Oh, that. Forget it." He shrugged, and a baked bean arced out of his sandwich and landed on the path. He stuffed the last couple of bites into his mouth and wiped his hands on his jersey. "So. FangMen."

At that moment I had a heart-stopping thought. What if the reporter wrote his article for a blog? And I never saw it?

A second later I thought, No. Someone would've said something. I was getting jumpy, that was all.

"That's a six," said Attila, interrupting himself to point at a tree.

"Course it is. It's always windier here."

He snorted, and hitched his bag further round his shoulder.

The Beaufort Scale's surprising. Its full name is the Beaufort Wind Force Scale. Here's the description of a Number 4 wind, a.k.a. a Moderate Breeze: *Raises dust and loose paper; small branches moved.*

And a Number 6, Strong Breeze: *Large branches in motion; whistling heard in overhead wires; umbrella use becomes difficult.*

I suppose someone needs to know this stuff. If they're out sailing, say, or trekking in the mountains.

The scale goes up to a 12, Hurricane: *Devastation.*

The Comet Show

Attila veered off for his place and I crossed the road, still wondering what had made me so wild.

I watched my feet go up the steps, passing familiar cracks. At the top my brain turned again to worst-case headlines. It was my new habit for this part of the walk home, as I got closer and closer to our letterbox and the newspaper.

SON WHINGES: "DADDY'S NOT A COWARD!!"
BLEATING BOY HUMILIATES FAMILY

I glanced down the street and stopped. Phoebe was outside their place, leaning against a tree. I'd have to walk right past.

A couple of days ago I'd have been pretty okay with that. But Phoebe was Boyd's sister. And Boyd drove cars at seven-year-olds.

I still wanted to walk past, though.

I focused on not falling over. Watching my feet seemed to help. When I was pretty close, Phoebe said, "Have you seen the new planetarium show? The comets one? It's primo."

I was so surprised I stopped and said, "Yeah, it is primo."

She was only Boyd's half-sister, after all.

Then a burning flush zoomed up my face. It wasn't just a mild reddening, it was catastrophic. I rushed past, grabbed the newspaper and pushed through our gate.

Inexplicably, Phoebe called after me, "See you round!"

I skulked out of sight under the trees until Phoebe went inside, then sagged onto the shed step. All the things I could have said started crowding in. Witty remarks. Amazing insights. Jokes.

At least the newspaper didn't have any braying headlines.

I sighed, and went inside.

There was something about the quiet in the sunroom.

Mum was bent over the coffee table, reading an outspread magazine. She looked up. "There's an article."

She seemed unsteady. I went closer, into the warmer air.

"About your father."

Her finger moved down a column, and stopped. She straightened and looked out the window.

The article had yellow and red pages, and photos of climbers I didn't recognize. A big red headline and black type. My eyes skipped from phrase to phrase.

FALLOUT CONTINUES, ONE YEAR ON
When James Theodorus, climbing guide ... world's highest mountain ... controversy ... surviving family's daily ... dysfunctional ... afflicted household ...

With no warning Mum yelled. "Where'd he *get* this?"

She was staring at me.

I opened my mouth, and shut it. Maybe if I told her everything. Maybe she'd understand. But I couldn't think how to start.

"I trusted her," said Mum.

What? "Who?"

"Jessica." She pushed around me for the door.

"No. Wait—wait. It's not Jessica."

She kept going, muttering.

"Mum."

She turned with an impatient frown.

"It was me."

Her face lost the frown. She took a couple of steps back, and sat on the couch.

"You?"

A few seconds later she said, "What have you done?"

Kablooey

"You talked to that … snake?"

Mum's mouth was all pushed out. She jabbed a wavering finger at the magazine. "You gave him that bullshit? That … dysfunctional crap?"

Even through my panic I was indignant. "Course not."

"Then where'd he get it?"

"I don't know."

She gripped her forehead. "What did you tell him?"

I didn't answer. Mum dropped her hand. "Well? What was it? 'Struggling to cope'? Or 'afflicted household'?" At full volume she yelled, "Which part was yours?"

My head hurt. "He just—he kept saying stuff. More and more stuff. And he pissed me off so much I got angry, and … I don't even know what I said." I pointed at the table. "Not that."

She got up. "I need to think." I listened to her walk down the hallway. Her bedroom door slammed, shaking the air.

The gate latch clinked. Five seconds later Fen came in, his face inscrutable. He must have heard. With a sideways glance at me he headed for his room. His door closed too.

It was the first article, right after the contents page, a double spread with perkily tilted pictures of mountaineers in goggles and snow suits. They stood with their legs braced on an unidentified mountain, and prayer flags and snow whipped in the background.

I threw the magazine. It hit the wall and slid down. Outside, Figaro crept belly to the ground, back low and straight and a twitch in the tip of his tail. I went to my room.

Some corner of my mind had been sneakily thinking that if an article did come out, it'd serve Mum right. Just a bit. For not standing up for Dad.

Got that wrong, then.

And here was a thought. Where had this crappy magazine come from? Mum wouldn't have bought it.

Zeustian Logic: Hey.

Karmic Pasty: yes

Zeustian Logic: Reporter did an article. About us. Theodoruses.

Karmic Pasty: what the hell/

serious?

Zeustian Logic: Says we're dysfunctional.

Karmic Pasty: dys what? who?

Zeustian Logic: Mum, me, Fen. Because of the accident.

Karmic Pasty: no way. what's the dys- thing even?

Zeustian Logic: Not operating normally or properly. Deviating from social norms blah blah blah

Karmic Pasty: crap on high

Serpens the Serpent

The first impression inside is red. There are long rows of tilt-backed red seats, and the carpet's red, and the planetarium dome itself is shades of orange and red. There's a strip of black around the walls that somehow makes the red even redder. Where the walls stop and the dome starts it's intense orange, but the further up you look, the lighter it gets, and at the top there's nothing to focus on so it's like staring at a hazy sunrise that goes on forever.

No one else turned up for the five o'clock session. The operator came onto the speakers and talked for a while, then started the projector. The show was about technological gadgets—smart phones, pacemakers, laser surgery—and how we have space research to thank for them all.

I only know because I've seen it before. I was there to think.

At first sight, the article looked bad. Of course.

But I'd started reasoning it through. Maybe it wasn't so terrible.

Mum's friends Laura and Jessica would come over. With tissues. They'd all sit around talking and having casseroles.

Mum would see that if she'd just talked to the reporter, none of this would've happened. If she'd just calmly said, "Well, actually, James Theodorus was a brilliant climber and a stellar guide and he wouldn't have done that to anyone, thanks very much ..." Well. Maybe she wouldn't be so upset right now.

And maybe talking to Laura and Jessica would make her realize she had to do something about her kids, who could actually use a bit of help with dishes and meals and stuff.

Maybe it'd be a wake-up call, all round.

I gave the seat in front of me a good thump. There was no way it'd be a good thing. I could just see the guys at school, looking over and snorting. The muttering at lunchtime. Anonymous heckles from a distance. Gentle slaps on the shoulder from teachers.

Then there was Fen. I'd seen his latest school report, saying he was withdrawn and needed to "engage more". This wouldn't help.

And Mum. She'd only ever wanted privacy.

All in all? Not my finest hour.

The show finished and the planetarium operator came back on. I made an effort to tune in.

"Serpens is the only one of the eighty-eight modern constellations with two separate parts." She paused, and a laser dot appeared on the screen. It started jiggling and looping around a group of stars.

"This is Serpens Caput, the head."

More wavery circling around another group.

"And this is Serpens Cauda, the tail. While in between—" much bigger, crazy loops— "holding both of them—this is Ophiuchus. The healer who started out as Asclepius."

I pushed myself up and along the row, bumping my knees, shoving chairs.

A bodiless voice squawked, "Excuse me. It's not finished. The night sky—"

I heaved the door open. It whuffed shut behind me, and her voice faded.

There was no sign of Mum in the kitchen or living room, or in the hallway. In my room I dithered, trying to decide whether to tell Fen. By six o'clock I still hadn't decided.

I zapped a couple of frozen dinners and we ate in the living room, not talking, just watching out the windows while the garden got darker. After a while I thought, to hell with it.

"Hey."

He looked up, chewing.

"Something's happened."

He stopped chewing.

I put my fork down. "Remember the moronic reporter?"

He nodded.

"He wrote something." I leaned to retrieve the magazine from the rack where I'd stashed it. Fen slid off the couch and came over.

I felt like a criminal. "It wasn't stuff I told him. Not on purpose. He made a lot of it up."

Fen looked at the yellow starburst stamped with TRAGEDY! in the top-right corner. He scanned the pages, breathing through his mouth. He sounded out, "Falling ... con—"

"Fallout," I said. "Like, effects. Results."

But he'd moved on. "The ... tra–gic ... events."

Then his finger skated abruptly downward, and landed on *Theodorus* a few lines lower. "James Theodorus."

"Yeah. It's about Dad. On the mountain. It's saying ... about everything that happened."

His finger carried on, trailing along a couple of lines and stopping on a photo of prayer flags. An oxygen canister was out of focus in the background.

The silence was getting to me. I poked the page. "It says Dad … couldn't save one of the people up there."

I paused, then spelled it out. "Didn't save."

Fen looked up, almost as far as my face but not quite. He took a breath. I braced myself.

He went back to the chair, scraped up the last of his chilli beans and put them in his mouth. He chewed, head down, watching his feet. Then he picked up his plate and took it to the kitchen bench.

Impressive, I thought cautiously.

But when he turned for his room, I could see it wasn't good at all. He looked more closed-up than ever.

Life Advice from
Patrick Ayms

The next morning, Fen and I were going out the door when Mum turned up and gave us both a hug. She didn't say anything, but as the door closed she waved through the gap. Fen waved back.

At the bus stop Attila tried to be nice. He opened his bag with a flourish and offered me a lunch-wrapped sandwich. "Sausage and sprouts."

I backed away. "Not a chance. But yeah, thanks."

He pushed the parcel in Fen's direction. "You?"

Fen managed a polite, "No, thank you," put his head down and made a beeline for the corner, his legs stomping and his bag jerking back and forth. Mrs Conrad's thumbs-up looked tentative.

The closer we got to school, the jumpier my guts felt.

"C'mon," said Attila. "No one'll give a toss. Trust me. Half of them won't even know. I mean—" he spread his hands and shrugged— "who reads those things anyway?"

A second later, he looked thoughtful.

"Hey, but let's just say for argument's sake someone does. Someone's mum. Or dad." He squinted around. "Maybe … they're at the supermarket, or getting fish and chips." He warmed to the story, walking faster, scratching his eyebrow. "So they come home, right? And they say something at dinner. Y'know, 'Guess what I saw at the chip shop today?' That kinda thing."

He stopped, looking triumphant. "Well. It goes the same place as everything else they say, yes?" He swished a finger across his throat. "Nowhere. Into the ether. In one ear—" he pointed at his ear— "out the other. Straight—"

"I get it," I said.

I just felt tired.

We were nearly at school when Attila said, "Hey. Outstanding name for a women's magazine."

I sighed. I really wasn't in the mood.

He snickered. "Woman's Monthly."

At the school gate, we skirted the crater in the asphalt and Attila started describing a scene from a web comic. A bunch of newbs were shuffling in circles nearby, talking their usual crap. One of them glanced over and gave a cut-off laugh, and the whole lot clustered inwards, hooting.

"What the hell?" I said.

Attila was mid-gesture. "Huh?"

I jerked my head. "That lot—heckling."

Attila glanced over, hands still in the air, and briefly narrowed his eyes. "Nah. It's newbs, remember? Blind to all but themselves." And he was off again.

At assembly the mood was nervy and lawless. My brain buzzed. Teachers kept yelling for quiet, but nothing worked. Heads swivelled, scuffles flared and there were outbreaks of smothered laughter until finally Mr Glenkin lost it and thumped the lectern, causing a screech of feedback. It triggered brief chaos, with a few high-pitched ooohs and some rapidly suppressed clapping.

Straggling back to the homeroom, I felt murderous. Attila was oblivious, still going on about the web comic. Finally I'd had enough. "That went well."

"Huh?"

"'No one'll give a toss'? It was a nuthouse in there."

He did his eyebrow quirk. "Yeah. Just like every other day."

But back in our room, people definitely ignored me.

Not that I'm typically surrounded by adoring fans. It was how careful they were about it. Joe Brenner did a quick mournful smile in my direction and ducked his head back into his book, while everyone else got unaccountably busy with their stuff. Or I'd look across and they'd be just that second looking away.

I got my books out and slapped them onto the desk.

Mrs Ziegler tromped down the veranda.

MRS ZIEGLER [CRASHES THROUGH DOOR, RIFLING THROUGH GREEN LEATHER SATCHEL]: Good morning.

CLASS MUMBLES RANDOM GREETINGS.

MRS ZIEGLER [BANGS SATCHEL ONTO DESK, STARES AROUND ROOM]: Let me come straight to the point. Gutter journalism is abhorrent, and should be treated with the contempt it deserves. [SCRATCHES HAIR] Right. Books out, page forty-seven.

At lunchtime Attila said, "Get a grip. It's all in your head."

He was on the back of the wooden bench, his shoes on the seat. He had a wary eye out for Mr Jones, who's been known to roar, "Feet off bloody seats!" the whole length of a playing field.

"Right," I said. "I get it. So. Gippo's crack about afflicted house-holds. That's in my head, is it?" I slammed my lunchbox. "Makes perfect sense. And—Smithers doing the air violin at break. That's in my head too, right?"

Attila frowned, and leaned back into mid-air. "Just don't get your daks in a flap." He launched forwards again, looking intense. "It's this week's story. Next week'll be something else. Why not enjoy it?" His eyes widened. "In actual—why not ham it up? Moan about your poor afflicted household. About how dys—" he scowled— "how messed up you are. Damn, make stuff up!"

I gave him a look. "Good. Thanks. Life advice from Patrick Ayms. Pretend you're more of a loser than you already are."

Attila rolled his eyes. "Fine," he muttered. "Trying to help."

"I don't want help," I said.

Later I said, "Jeez. Whatever. Sorry."

"Yeah, no worries, but hey. Been thinking about FangMen. Had another brainwave."

I sighed. "And?"

"LemurWomen."

This Week's Story

The rest of the day passed without serious drama. People gawped in corridors and along verandas, but there were only a couple of actual jeers, one hooted from the toilet block and the other out on the playing field.

Trudging home with Attila, I felt weary.

We went round by the rose gardens, so Attila could get a lime cola from the one shop in the entire city that stocks the brand he likes. The sun came out, lighting up the metal sculptures on the hill, and as we scraped through orange and yellow leaves in the grass I started feeling less stupefied. Even a bit hopeful.

Maybe Attila was right. Maybe tomorrow would be better.

By next week, everything might have blown over.

"… along the lines of werewolves," said Attila, continuing the monologue he'd started at the classroom door. "But … more. Not just—y'know—" he looked scornful— "fangs an' full moons an' crap. It'll be more … dunno. Surreal." He gazed skyward, looking rapt. "Werewolves with a twist. It'll be great."

After the shop we took the track up to the Met building, and past there to the observatory and cable car. The city looked blue.

Later, at the turn-off, Attila said, "You coming over?"

I shrugged. "Yeah, nah. Thanks, though."

He nodded and thumped my shoulder. "Tomorrow, my compatriot."

At home I went straight to the kitchen for a sludge and took it out to the sunroom, eating it off a soup spoon because nothing else was clean.

A couple of blackbirds bounced around the lawn, stalking worms. I felt bad for the worms. They couldn't be particularly happy, with a big beady eye in a twitchy head peering down at their private lives.

Afterwards I looked in Fen's room, but he wasn't there.

He wasn't with Mum either, which was no surprise since she was asleep in her chair.

I went outside to check if he was hanging around with Figaro under the trees. He sometimes does that.

A school sports thing, maybe? Late from a class trip? I went back along the street, down the steps and across to the school.

It was mostly deserted, except for the after-school group in the hall and one or two kids riding scooters. On the far side of the playground, in the sandpit, a couple of pre-schoolers were bickering over a blue digger while two women talked nearby.

One of the scooter riders looked about Fen's age, so I went over.

"Hi. You seen Fen Theodorus?"

He shook his head.

"Sure?"

He kept shaking his head. His eyes got bigger, and rounder.

"Okay," I said. "Thanks anyway."

He scuttled away, pushing the scooter ahead of him on ramrod-straight arms.

It took twenty minutes of scouring the place, but I found him. He was in the adventure playground, crammed in behind a climbing wall of lashed-together tyres.

"What—?" I hunched down in the clay. "You okay?"

He didn't look up.

"Hey. What's wrong?"

He did a miserable shrug, and fresh tears went down the tracks on his cheeks.

"Hey, c'mon." I shuffled closer to the tyres. "It's okay." I reached through a gap, but he leaned away.

"Look—hang on—"

It wasn't easy, but I squeezed my way in next to him. Instantly my school jersey was a mess of mud and black stuff. Fen moved a fraction to one side, making room.

"Now," I said, finally in, puffing. "What's all this?"

He shifted, and I smelled something sour.

He'd peed himself.

It took a few seconds, but I recovered.

"Hey, you had an accident. So what? Don't worry about it."

He shook his head.

"It happens," I said.

He shook his head harder.

"Tell you what." I tugged at my jersey. "You wear this."

He frowned at it, not understanding.

"It'll come over your knees," I said. "No one'll see. C'mon. I'll go out there. Take it off. Pass it in." I looked out, and had another inspiration. "We'll go the back way."

He looked up. His eyebrows were tragic. He gave a small nod.

"Right," I said in a hurry, thinking he might change his mind. "Gimme a sec."

I squeezed out again, pulled the jersey off, turned it right-side-out and pushed it back in. "Shove your bag out."

He took forever, squirming around getting the thing on, while I hovered outside. When he was finally ready, I climbed the tyres to check the playground.

"Coast's clear," I hissed.

We were out of there in no time, and around the back of the caretaker's place, and from there it was a fast dash to the side street. I held his bag sort of draped around his other side. It only took a minute to get across the road and up the steps.

At the end of our street I said, "Get you a bath when we're home." He nodded and kept walking. "Bubbles," I added.

He did a faint grin.

A white car was parked outside our place. It had something on the side, a logo and words, but it was too far away to read.

Boyd came out of next door's garage, holding pliers and a rag. He looked our way and sauntered down the drive towards the road, a bit faster than usual. I shifted Fen to my other side.

At the end of the drive Boyd stopped. Fen and I pulled up too.

"You got visitors," said Boyd. The pliers clacked open and shut.

Fen bumped my side and whispered, "I want to go in."

I started off again, keeping an eye on Boyd.

He watched us pass. "Social Services, eh?"

Social Services

I smothered the latch with my shirt and squeezed the gate shut.

Social Services. I had an idea they helped sick people and old people. But maybe also families whose fathers died on mountains?

Fen clearly had questions too. His eyes were dark and goggly. "Round the back," I muttered. I didn't feel like meeting strangers. Fen pulled the jersey around his legs and followed.

Unfortunately, we had to sneak along the front path.

I went first, hunched over like a secret agent, and there, right by the open door, was Social Services, a shortish woman wearing a blue dress and looking unhappy. Mum was there too, further inside. Neither of them had seen us.

I eased back, nudging Fen behind me.

"What does a *concerned parent*," I heard Mum say in the slow, ominous voice she uses with reporters if she isn't screaming at them, "know about this family?"

"I understand it must be upsetting," said the woman.

"Which *concerned parent* was it? Anyone I know?"

Everything went quiet.

"Well, of course," the woman said, "I'm not able—"

"What did they say?" Mum sounded scornful. "Because I'm wondering if their concerns might owe something to trashy sensationalism?"

There was another silence. The social worker started talking again, more quietly. I could barely hear. I looked around at Fen. He was staring into the trees, daydreaming.

"… disturbing drawings," the woman murmured.

Mum didn't answer.

The woman said something I couldn't hear, then, "… very withdrawn". And a bit later, "… obsessive behaviour. Counting, symmetry … rearranging his possessions …" Then I heard, "risk of self-harm".

Fen was still gazing up, still vacant. Turning back, I heard the woman mutter, "… quite concerned."

Nothing from Mum.

In a hissy whisper right at my elbow, Fen said, "Who is it?"

"Shh."

The woman stepped towards the doorway, and the light came onto her face. She looked nice. She had dark straight hair and a friendly smile.

Fen leaned against me. The woman's smile had just moved onto him, and was starting to change to puzzlement about his enormous jersey, when into my head popped a picture of the kid who moved away when I was ten or eleven. Archie someone.

He'd gone to a foster family, we heard, because his mother left and his father couldn't look after him.

I shoved in front of Fen, almost knocking him over.

"Hi!" I crossed my arms. Fen's bag fell off my shoulder. I grabbed for it and slung it over my other shoulder. "We're just … heading out, uh, round the back."

97

Why? Why were we? *Think!*

"… 'cause there's a, like, a—cat. Figaro. The cat. He belongs next door. He's insane." I looped a finger near my ear. "So, y'know, we'll just—" I shambled left, hands behind me shuffling Fen along— "… find the cat."

Fen tripped. I whipped around, grabbed him and hoisted him out of sight behind a potted shrub.

A few seconds later I leaned back around the shrub. Mum and the woman were watching with identical bewildered frowns.

I caught up with Fen and nudged him past the sunroom, along the veranda to the living-room window. We leaned forward.

Empty.

Maybe Mum was keeping the woman at the door. Maybe she'd used her old trick and sent her away. We ducked under the window and went on hands and knees to the corner.

"Stay here." I crept along to the east-facing windows.

Mum and the woman were going into the living room. Their mouths were moving. They navigated the coffee table and sat, shifting cushions. Mum took the red chair facing me and leaned forward, studying the woman's every word.

I sneaked back to the corner.

"I want to go in," said Fen.

"We have to wait."

"Why?"

"When the lady goes," I hissed, "we can go in."

I got a whiff of pee and glanced down. He was quivering. "Fine. We'll go in. Just—" I grabbed his shoulder— "don't let her see you're wet."

He nodded, already pushing past me.

Of course he went straight to Mum, the little sneak, and stuffed himself into the chair beside her. Mum draped an arm absently along his shoulders.

The Social Services woman stood and moved around the coffee table. Fen watched, clutching the jersey against him. She held out her hand. "Hello. I'm Celia. You must be Fenton." After a few seconds Fen's hand inched out of the folds of jersey. Celia smiled down at him, shaking his hand up and down. "I'm very pleased to meet you." She turned her head. "And you would be Duncan?"

I shrugged.

Celia went back to the couch, picking up a pen and a blue and brown folder from the table. She put her hands on the folder on her knees and looked around at us all. I saw her thoughtful glance at my lack of jersey. "If we could just have a quick chat."

Mum sat up taller. Fen whimpered and pushed in under her armpit. "Just to see how you're all doing," said Celia.

"I'm sorry." Mum didn't look it. "What's the process here?"

Celia held up the pen. "It's nothing to worry about at this—"

"Sorry," said Mum again. "I've changed my mind. It's not a good time." She started getting up. Fen squealed.

"Rose," said Celia. "Please, stay calm. There's—"

Mum pointed towards the front door.

Celia blinked. "This attitude ..."

Mum didn't answer. After a moment, Celia reached under the coffee table and pulled out her bag. She followed Mum through the kitchen. A few seconds later the front door closed.

The pen was still on the coffee table.

Mum came back, and Fen scuttled over to her.

She crouched and pushed his hair back. "What's the matter?" Then she sniffed the air, and gave me a disbelieving look over his head. "I *thought* I smelled—has he—"

I nodded.

"Oh, no. Fen, love, are you all right?"

A second later she looked up. "You think she saw?"

I nodded. "I tried to get him to—y'know. Get a bath. But he wanted you." Fen squeezed his arms tighter around her.

"The article?" she muttered. "He knows?"

I nodded, feeling guilty. But it reminded me. And I thought I should make the most of Mum being so unusually talkative. "Where'd you get the magazine?"

She frowned. "In the letterbox. Rolled up—a piece of paper around it. Someone must've put it there." She glanced out the window. "They'd put 'Mouse' on it."

Fen looked up from her shoulder, snuffling. "There was a mouse?"

"No," said Mum. "Just the word. Mouse."

Closure

So. Boyd put the magazine in the letterbox. Maybe he even helped write the article. Maybe he gave the reporter lots of juicy stuff. No wonder he was so keen to see us get home.

I felt weird. On my bedroom windowsill, the plasticine Beast stared out as always from the Lego drawbridge and ramparts. I'd toiled over that thing for hours, or maybe days, prodding and squeezing the plasticine into the right shapes. I remembered clutching it all the way home from school, and placing it in the precise spot for defending the castle.

I started noticing other stuff. The cricket ball on the windowsill too, bleached red with tattered dirty-white stitching. And under that, a birthday card from a kid who left a long time ago for a different school.

I heard distant murmuring from Mum, and answering chirps from Fen, and the far-off splashing of water. That was something. It was a long time since she'd supervised one of Fen's baths.

The red plastic box under the desk overflowed as always with amputee Lego creatures, random limbs, weapons, helmets and green staring eyes. Overhead, the solar system swayed in an air current. Dad and I made it from a kitset when I was ten or eleven. Looking up, I remembered painting Jupiter's spot and how slow and painful it was, and how proud I was when it was done.

I wondered what Attila was doing.

At least he could be trusted not to pack us off to a foster home. Or make us write letters.

Zeustian Logic: Hey, you there?
Spiky Tarmac: howzit
Zeustian Logic: What're you doing?
Spiky Tarmac: perishing of hunger. starving in my shoes. what are they thinking? it's after SIX young men need feeding. am i right? nourishment yes?

What would Attila think, I wondered, if he knew how often dinner appeared at six at my place? More importantly, what if I told him it was Boyd who put the magazine in the letterbox?

It wasn't worth it. He'd go off on an epic rant, then dream up some crazy, tangled plan of vengeance. The kind of thing Mrs Ziegler calls his ruses and machinations.

Spiky Tarmac: hey. been thinking
a thing that might help.
maybe find out more.
yknow. about what happened
up there on the mountain.
it's bugging you, yes?
so find out more.
it's what they say—
CLOSURE, yes? all that?

Attila's grandmother used to be a psychologist, and over the years he's gleaned some useful stuff. Just at that moment I wasn't interested.

Spiky Tarmac: hey. you there?
Zeustian Logic: How the hell am I supposed to find out more?
Spiky Tarmac: ah well, you see
Zeustian Logic: —hire a detective?
Spiky Tarmac: hold on
Zeustian Logic: —fly to NEPAL?
Spiky Tarmac: would you just
Zeustian Logic: —go round interviewing everyone?
Spiky Tarmac: hey
Zeustian Logic: —shove a microphone in people's noses?
Spiky Tarmac: think you might be ready to listen?
Zeustian Logic: No chance.
Spiky Tarmac: so here's the idea.
find a few people round here
who were there. on the mountain.
must be one or two, am i right?
and then ... talk to em.
ask about it. have chats.
and with any luck:
kazoom shazam
closured up.
sorted.
yes?

Jeez. I suppose he means well.

Asclepius, a.k.a. Ophiuchus

Maybe Attila was right. Maybe I should talk to someone. Someone who was there, on the mountain.

I had talked to Mike, of course—way back when it happened. I remembered him at our gate, describing what happened on the mountain, and how tired and upset he'd looked. Not to mention how I felt. Who'd want to do that again? It was why I'd never talked to anyone else. Not Mum. Not Great Aunt Mintie, although she tried a couple of times. Definitely not the counsellor.

But you never knew. Someone might have seen something important. They might not even have realized it was important. They might know the thing, but not know how crucial it was. Talking about it might jog their memory, and they might suddenly remember something incredibly significant.

They might figure out that everything happened completely differently from how they all thought.

I scribbled a list of everyone on the expedition. They'd all been to our house at one time or another: the guides, the new clients, the repeat client who'd got sick on her first try and wanted to go back.

Adrian, the team doctor, who everyone said had magic hands.

A couple of them, Sarah and David, I only knew by their first names. Tracking them down was unlikely. If only their parents had thought to give them names like Zebediah or Latifah. I went online for clues.

Buried twelve pages back was a photo on a blog.

Dad's hat was off. His dark hair had gone crazy, and his eyes were scrunched up so the lines spread out from them. He was lifting his axe in one hand, and in the other, which was blurry with movement, were his hat and goggles. It was obvious from the way he stood that he wanted to get going.

They were all lined up in their bright climbing gear in the churned snow, grinning and squinting. The second-try woman rubbed her forehead with a big orange glove. The doctor, whose red hair stuck straight up and out, had both blue-mittened hands held up behind someone's ears.

My eyes went from face to face, but always back to Dad.

Their full names were listed, and their home cities. And surprise surprise, the only one within halfway practical distance was Mike. Though it wasn't that surprising, really, considering he'd been Dad's business partner.

I had pretty strong memories of Meg and Mike's old house. But they'd moved to somewhere in the Hutt Valley not long before the accident, and we'd never been out to see them there.

It'd be a trek. Walk. Bus. Train. Walk. Then reverse.

I tapped the pencil holder. I could email him instead. If I could find the address. But what would I say?

"Excuse me. I wonder if you'd be able to help me discover the triumphant news that Dad didn't, in fact, abandon a client on Mount Everest. Yours sincerely, Tuttle." Ridiculous.

Or I could phone him. But it'd be the same thing. "Hi, it's Tuttle, I just thought you might've changed your mind about Dad deserting Stephen Pritcher, what d'you think?"

All in all, pretty pointless.

To have even the slightest chance of success, I'd have to see him in person. The best thing would be to turn up without warning. So he wouldn't have time to figure out what to say. Turn up, and ask him straight: What happened up there? And—isn't it possible it wasn't what everyone says? I'd watch his face while he told me what he knew.

Maybe it was the only way.

Maybe there really would be a kazoom shazam moment.

Their address was online under Culver, M&M.

It wouldn't be easy—sneaking out and sneaking in again. It'd take a couple of hours at least. Mum might notice. And to have a chance of getting to Silverstream before nine or ten p.m., I'd have to rush Fen into bed. I could hear him, plodding around the house in bare feet.

Something smelled like dinner. Mum was cooking.

We ate at the kitchen table. Everyone was quiet but oddly calm. It reminded me of the mood after Gam's funeral, when everyone seemed to need a break from being sad.

I tried not to think about Celia from Social Services. Or Boyd, or the article. Or Mike.

I was crunching into my last bite of lasagne when cunning inspiration struck. I thought about it for a while.

"I might head down to the observatory."

Mum nodded.

"I'll do Fen's story first," I said. "If you settle him down later?"

In the past few months I hadn't asked Mum for help once, and she looked slightly stunned. "Of course." She actually smiled. "You're working on a project?"

I sort of nodded and sort of shrugged. "Project" is a broad word.

Mum reached for the plates and forks, still smiling. I pointed at Fen. "Right. Story."

He started to object, but I talked over him. "You can play afterwards—you'll be in bed, that's all." I scraped my chair back and stood, acting brisk and businesslike. "C'mon, let's make it snappy. I've got stuff to do."

He got down off his chair. He was frowning, but he was going.

I felt bad. But it was for a good cause.

The climbing doctor was still on my mind, so when Fen was in bed I gave him a quick version of the story of Asclepius, the guy in Greek mythology who was so good at healing he started bringing people back from the dead.

"Zeus was impressed," I said, "but he was also conflicted. He didn't really want humans getting immortality. Besides, Hades had started complaining he was losing clients."

Fen's eyelids flickered. Strange. It was nowhere near his bedtime but he looked ready to conk out.

"So," I said, quieter. "Zeus nuked Asclepius with a thunderbolt and put him in the sky as a constellation called Ophiuchus."

His eyelids drooped.

I went on. "Like, 'You're amazing, dude, but sorry, can't let you carry on, so TAKE THAT.'"

His eyes opened. I continued. "And then he said, 'Actually, you were so amazing I'll make you into a constellation!'" I leaned forward. "Like a big consolation prize."

I waited a suitable interval, and delivered the punchline in a whisper. "Constellation prize, geddit?"

Attila would've been proud. Fen didn't even register. His eyes stayed open maybe two seconds, then he was out.

What I hadn't mentioned was that Asclepius had a daughter named Hygiene.

What was he thinking?

Orion the Hunter

The steps down to Glenmore Street made a gloomy, jagged row, long and steep, but a smell of frying onions near the top took the spooky edge off. It was almost seven-thirty.

Usually I'm home from the observatory by eleven. If Mum checks up on me, it's around then. With luck I'd be back in time.

Our place to the railway station is easy, and I'd memorized the route from there. Silverstream station to Whiteman's Road looked like ten minutes' walk. Fifteen at the most.

I crossed the road to the bus shelter, checked the timetable, and looked up for my bearings.

Antares was there, the big red heart of Scorpius, and, further over, Altair and the rest of the Eagle. Roughly in between was Serpens Cauda, the tail of the Serpent.

Ophiuchus is hard to see, not having any bright stars, but it's got some interesting things—Barnard's Star, the fastest-moving star in the whole sky, and the Eagle Nebula, which sounds like it should be in the Eagle constellation but isn't.

The number 3 bus pulled in. I found a seat near the front, and watched the stops go past till we got to the Quay. From there it's a quick walk to the train station. I bought a ticket, found a seat in an empty carriage, and wedged myself into the corner.

Along with the route, I'd tried to memorize what I'd say to Mike. The trouble was, it kept changing.

The main thing, first, was to get his sympathy. So, something along the lines of, "It's been pretty hard since …" or "There's something I want to know …" or "D'you reckon you could help …"

They were all too wimpy. They'd leave me wide open to "No," and "Sorry," and a closing door.

The train jolted. The eerily lit station glided backwards, and the walking people kept walking but went backwards anyway, and others sat on backwards-sliding benches watching us go.

It was now or never. Ready or not.

But I wasn't ready. And in half an hour I'd be on the spot.

I leaned on the glass. The sea was black except for a few little boats and the shaky lines of light they made on the water. Overhead between clouds were three stars in a row, and looking up, I got a vivid memory of drawing Orion with Dad.

I must have been pretty young, because I hadn't started going to the kids' astronomy club. We were out the back of our place, looking at stars from the lawn. "What are those?" I'd asked. "There—one, two, three?"

"Ah," said Dad. "Orion. The Great Hunter. Those are his belt."

I stared upward and the Great Hunter took shape around the three dots. A massive body. Chain mail. A raised arm with a big sword. And a victorious expression. I was hooked.

Later that night Dad came and found me. He was waving a piece of black cardboard and a little paintbrush, and he'd got a tube of white paint from Mum. He mixed paint with a few drops of water, and sat me down at the low table in the living room.

He'd printed a map of the Orion constellation—except it was black stars on a white sky. It was the first time I'd seen one of those, and I didn't like it. Also, as far as I could see, the Great Hunter was just a couple of warped squares joined along one crooked edge with a few random stars thrown around. Someone had drawn lines between the bigger stars and decided to call it Orion. It was nothing like the picture in my head.

Dad stirred the paint and got a drop on the end of the brush. I watched, feeling alarmed, as he leaned over the black cardboard and put down a blob of white. It sat, glistening.

"There. Betelgeuse. See?" He reached across to the page of black dots, pointing. Then he held out the brush. "Why don't you put in Bellatrix?"

I looked at the white blob.

"It doesn't have to be perfect. Here. Just follow the map."

I still hesitated, frowning over the black-star map. Maybe to reassure me or just to distract me, Dad said, "The stars in his belt. They look close together. But they're a very, very long way apart."

Jeez. I hope I knew that much.

"And the middle star," he said, "is a long, long way further from us than the other two are." He stretched his paintbrush hand way out behind him, and his other hand way forward in front of him, and sort of lined them up so the far one was almost hidden by the front one. "See?" He looked insanely pleased. "They seem close together. But they're far apart."

I didn't get it.

I get it now. Just so you know.

Eventually I managed a big quivery blob for Bellatrix. It smeared, but Dad said it was fine. Then he did Saiph. "Now," he said. "You do Rigel. It's the brightest."

I did Rigel and we put in a few others, too, checking against the black-star map. Dad went to get some pencils, and while he was gone I looked out the window, but I couldn't see Orion.

"Now," said Dad, back and crouching at the table. "The Hunter. Different people draw him differently."

I already knew that, from the stupid twisted squares.

"Sometimes," he said, "Betelgeuse and Bellatrix are his shoulders." He sketched a faint blue line between the two stars. "But sometimes Betelgeuse is further up his arm. Towards his elbow." He moved the pencil, and did a pale circle around Rigel. "Sometimes Rigel's his foot, and Saiph's his other thigh. Or sometimes they're both knees. Or both feet. Sometimes—" he rolled his eyes— "he's even drawn facing around the other way. With his back to us."

My head was spinning.

"So." Dad handed me the pencil. "Let's draw him how we want, eh?"

I gave Orion a massive sword, a big clumpy shoe for his Rigel foot, and when Dad pointed out the curved shape, a giant shield.

Of course he also had a spectacular belt. I went and got a red pencil for that.

It wasn't till later I found out that Orion's actually upside down in our sky. I suppose Dad didn't want to completely blow my mind.

Mike

The walk from Silverstream station was even shorter than I expected. The long driveway to Mike and Meg's house had lights, but they were solar and starting to fade, and some weren't working anyway. The cracks in the cobbles bulged with grass.

I stood on a welcome mat under a yellow downlight for a long time, shuffling. Off in the trees a morepork hooted.

I heard shouting inside, getting closer.

"So I'll take it *now*."

Something banged.

"Though *why*—" even louder, with another bang— "taking out the recycling is your idea of doing something around the house—" jerky clanking and rattling— "beats the hell out of me!"

The door was yanked open, and Mike stood holding a lumpy blue bag in one hand. His hair was longer and he had a beard.

"Bloody hellfire!" He took a step back, then came forward with a confused frown. "Tuttle? What the hell?"

"Sorry," I said. "Sorry. I just, I wanted—"

Good start.

"I need to talk to you. Ask you about ... Dad."

He dropped the bag and pulled the door wider. "Come in here—come in."

I stepped up into the house.

Mike gave me a quick, hard hug. His shirt smelled like curry. "It's bloody late. What the hell're you—this time of night?" He looked bewildered, but he was sort of grinning too. He shoved the plastic bag to one side and shut the door.

"Through there." He nudged me in front of him, towards brighter light around a corner.

The living room was a big wide space with a chimney in the middle. The curry smell was stronger. Meg was halfway up out of a reclining chair, like someone had pressed the remote. She saw me and slowly straightened.

"Look what the owl sent in," said Mike. He went to the sink, pushing up his sleeves, and I saw the end of the rope tattoo that twists up his arm.

Meg made a big fuss. She poured tea from a pot, and added two spoons of sugar and kept stirring it. Mike leaned on the bench and rubbed his elbow, staring off to the side like he always does. His hands were beat up with old scars from climbing.

Meg put milk in my tea and stirred it, and licked the teaspoon. I'd forgotten she did that.

It hit me how long it had been since our sunroom at home was filled with people drinking beer and cracking jokes. Or since we'd all been at the Gardens, for a picnic behind the café—or at a summer show at the sound shell.

The familiarity of them made me suddenly, peculiarly happy. Meg and Mike. They'd help. They'd have answers. I started talking, kind of fast, about the train trip and how the guy in the carriage had gone to sleep with his head drooped right over, and how there were more moreporks (ha ha) in Silverstream than in town, and so on and so on, until Meg handed me my tea and I realized I was blathering.

We went to chairs at the fireplace and settled, Meg saying little chatty things about the fire and the weather. Mike was quieter than I remembered.

There was a pause.

"So," said Mike. "What's this about?"

"Don't push him," said Meg.

"He's here for a reason. Let's hear it."

Meg leaned over and pressed my arm. "If there's anything we can do. We think of you all, Tut. Every day." She was looking really sad. "Every day."

I still hadn't worked out what to say. In the end I just opened my mouth and started talking in the hope I'd think of something.

"I just wanted to know about ... what happened. I mean, maybe something happened. Like I mean, something I didn't know about. Or maybe—someone else didn't know about."

I wasn't making any sense. I could hear it. I just couldn't fix it. "Did anyone maybe, say something—maybe afterwards—they might've remembered ..." I stopped. "Did anyone say anything?"

The room was quiet. Meg gripped her mug and looked even sadder. "You're asking about your dad."

I managed a nod.

She gave Mike a helpless look, and sighed. "We don't know anything more, do we? Than we did a year ago. Nothing more."

Mike was watching the fire. He put a finger in his ear and scratched. No one said anything for a while. He shook his head. "Nothing more."

I nodded again, a few times.

Mike pulled off one of his shoes and used it to push a cinder towards the fireplace. He put all his concentration into it, squinting in the light from the fire. Finally he said, "It's much worse for you and Rose. And Fen. Of course."

"Mike?" said Meg.

He was hunched over and his voice was muffled. "But sometimes you have to just … move on."

"Mike!" said Meg. "The poor boy."

He talked over her. "You have to move on."

Meg made annoyed *tsk* noises and breathed hard through her nose. Mike ignored her. He was scraping again, but slower.

Then he looked up and I guess he saw my face. "Well. It's tough. Just—it's tough on all of us."

Meg thumped her mug onto the chair arm, frowning.

Pretty soon after that, Mike said they'd drive me to the station. He seemed keen to get going. I gulped my tea.

"Does Rose know you're here?" said Meg. I shook my head, and she gave me a half-exasperated, half-worried look. Mike rattled his keys.

Meg talked a lot on the trip, all about living in the valley—how the traffic wasn't as bad as in town, how they had a great local baker but the supermarket was expensive, how the weather was always better than in the city. I watched the street lights go past.

We pulled in at the station and Mike cut the engine. Meg leaned between the seats to pat my knee. "It's been such a treat to see you, Tuttle. I hope you'll keep in touch."

I made a vague noise that wasn't yes and wasn't no.

Meg looked at Mike. He sat straighter, and nodded in the rear-view mirror. "Good to see you, Tut. Got your ticket?"

I held it up.

"Good. All the best then." He looked out the front. "Sorry we couldn't be more helpful."

I got out.

Meg kept waving as the car turned in the gravel and left.

After the dark of the station, everything on the train gleamed. I slid across to the window and kicked my bag under the seat.

How could Mike not remember anything? There must be something he could have said. As far as I could see, he was too busy being grumpy at Meg.

The train lurched, gently rocked and started, and the pale-yellow station lights slid away. A guy in a high-vis vest watched us go. It was a bit after ten.

Mum wouldn't be expecting me yet, but I was cutting it fine.

All the way back to town, useless snips of thoughts went through my head. I barely noticed the walk from the station to the Quay. The number 3 bus rolled up ten minutes late and it was a trolley again, which meant a slow trip up the hill.

I stood in the aisle, rocking with the bus and alternating between anger at the pointless trip and worry at getting home late. If Mum rang the observatory, I'd be toast. At my stop I rocketed up the steps with so much energy I wasn't even puffing at the top. Upland Road didn't see me for dust. It was almost eleven.

I squeezed the door shut and pushed off my shoes.

Something bumped in the living room. Uh oh. A second later Mum appeared at the kitchen door, looking accusing. "I was starting to worry."

"Sorry." I didn't feel sorry. I was pretty done with adults.

Mum was still frowning. "Not everyone gets to go out late, looking at stars. It's a privilege, remember. Not a right."

I nodded, nudging my shoe around.

Mum kept talking, and I scrutinized my shoes and decided to go back online. See what I could ferret out. Starting with the radio podcast—maybe I'd missed something.

"Now goodnight." Mum went off down the hallway. A sigh came back over her shoulder.

I woke the computer, found the page and listened to the podcast again—this time, right to the end. But, no. The climber named John did not think it was okay to abandon someone on Mount Everest. Not under any circumstances.

I did see one thing, though. At the bottom there was a link to a mountaineering forum. I clicked through and looked around.

Cynth33a: So why go up there? What's so good about choking for air, feeling like puke and falling down a crevasse? Thanking my lucky stars I don't have that drive lol.
JoeOh6: Agreed. Not for the fainthearted.

I scrolled down.

Bootzwench: Who are you guys - - - mountain police? Why shouldn't they go up? You gonna stop em? Sure - - - it's no picnic up there, you gotta know your limits. But it's no one else's business if you go or stay.

There was more. A lot more. I scrolled past screeds—essays. Dozens, hundreds of entries, sliding by in a long blurry rant.

So many opinions.

Attila's avatar flashed at the bottom of the screen. With a hard poke I shut the podcast tab.

Skimpy Carat: hey

Zeustian Logic: What.

Skimpy Carat: Non-Chosen novel.

bit tougher than expected. not going as planned.

i mean don't get me wrong: got 2K words. just not sure,
yknow ... what's happening.

Zeustian Logic: And?

Skimpy Carat: and—you got brainwaves? eureka
eye-openers? bright ideas, all the stuff Mrs Z goes on & on
about? she's always, yknow, plot, crap like that & you're
the one who listens, yes?

Zeustian Logic: How would I know?

Keep going, I guess.

I looked out the window for a while and saw a shooting star and a
couple of satellites.

I'd keep going with the forum comments. There had to be
something useful in there.

Lycaon the Werewolf

Heading down our street the next morning, I tried to figure out Fen's mood.

"You all right? Going back to school and everything?" I didn't want to mention the playground incident.

He gave a tetchy nod. At the bus shelter he took off without a glance, and a few seconds later rounded the school corner. Mrs Conrad clopped hurriedly after him. She'd forgotten her thumbs-up.

I thought of telling Attila about Silverstream and Mike. For moral support, and so on. But only for the micro-second it took to remember his ideas about revenge on Boyd. Anyway, he'd already launched into the Non-Chosen Novel.

"I don't get it. It's not rocket science. Why can't I do it?"

"I don't know. Mrs Ziegler's the English teacher. Ask her."

"Not a chance. I don't want a seminar." He swung his bag off his shoulder, unzipped the front pocket and pulled out a bread roll with something—bacon? tomato? *tongue?*—poking out the side. He unwrapped one end and bit into it, still talking. "She'd still be going a week later. She'd be so happy someone'd asked, she'd …"

I tuned him out. I had stuff to mull over. Like what Mum was thinking about the magazine. And whether I'd find Fen, wet and smelly, behind the tyres after school.

Attila was talking werewolves.

"… have to be a full moon, or is—say, seven-eighths enough?"

No point, of course, in wondering if there'd be further heckling at school. Of course there would.

"… fur?" said Attila. "… I mean, wolves, y'know, there's grey, and—that's about it. Doesn't leave a lot of room for …"

I remembered Mike glaring at the fire, or talking over Meg. And the car pulling away from the train station with me none the wiser.

"… what happens to the fur after…"

On top of all that, the forum comments kept swilling around in my head.

Attila had gone as quiet as me.

It made things easier, I decided. Less risk of distraction from one of his rants. Then it started to bug me. Attila quiet was freaky. Was he annoyed I wasn't listening? Usually he didn't even notice.

"What?" I said.

He glanced sideways. "Yeah, nothin'."

A bit later he glanced again.

"*What?*"

He shrugged. "Just. Y'know. Cheer up. Don't get your gruts in a bunch, kinda thing."

I stopped. "Easy for you."

He stopped too. "Well, y'know. It's not the end of the world."

I felt my forehead heating up. "Not for you, maybe."

"I mean—" He waved the bread-roll hand. "In the scheme of things." He looked almost pleading.

I sighed.

We started walking again.

I probably was being annoying, whingeing all the time and not bothering to talk. Especially when he was so excited about the Non-Chosen Novel. I decided to make a peace offering.

"I saw a thing about the first werewolf."

He stuffed the last, huge chunk of bread roll into his mouth.

"It's all mixed up with Ursa Major," I said. "The Great Bear."

He grunted and rolled his eyes, chewing. "Ancient Greeks for a change, then."

I ignored that. "It was a guy called Lycaon."

"What was?"

"The first werewolf, you dozo."

He blinked, and nodded rapidly.

"But before he was a werewolf, he was a king. In Greece. And he decided to set a challenge for Zeus. So one day, they were up at the sacrificial altar hanging out having a drink, and he—"

"Wait. Don't tell me. I got this." He swallowed with a gulp. "This is it, right?" He opened his arms wide. "One of 'em leans back on the barby, and he says—he says—'This is a great beer!' Right? Am I right? *Great beer?*" He looked triumphant.

I nodded with grudging approval and went on.

"So. They were up at the sacrificial altar, and Lycaon wanted to give Zeus a challenge. So—get this—he grabbed his own grandson and put him on the altar. Right in the fire."

Attila narrowed his eyes. I nodded. "And he said to Zeus, 'Let's see how clever you are—here, save my grandson.'"

"No way. What'd Zeus do?"

"Well. The kid was actually his son." I saw his expression. "Yeah, long story. Zeus had a thing with Lycaon's daughter."

Attila whistled. "Zeus. All the babes."

"So anyway, he saved the little kid. But then he turned Lycaon into a werewolf. For punishment."

Attila stared off down the street. I could see ideas galloping around in his head.

We'd just rounded the corner when suddenly, Phoebe was there. She had the silver zodiac thing around her neck. She veered around us and around the corner, and before I knew it she'd gone.

"Hey," said Attila. "Boyd's half-sister. Yes?"

I shrugged.

His eyebrows streaked up around his hairline. He had the beginnings of a big, annoying grin. "She gave you a look."

"Crap." I started walking fast. "No way."

"Oh yes she did," he said. He jogged to keep up, looking gleeful. "Definitely. A look. No doubt about it."

I shook my head. "Probably thinking about something else."

But it didn't help my concentration one bit.

Near the school gate a couple of older students homed in, aiming their paths to cross ours. The shorter one had slicked-back hair. He said, "You still dysfunctional, Theodorus?"

The taller one snorted.

Slicked-back said, "Gotta watch that erectile dysfunction!"

They veered off, laughing.

"Forget about it," said Attila. "They're losers."

I didn't answer.

"Idiots," said Attila.

I didn't answer.

"Don't take it so hard."

The bell rang.

In geography Attila leaned over to poke me with his ruler. "Hey. About the great bear."

I swung round. "You still on about that? Lousiest pun ever."

He looked confused, then shook his head. "No—Lycaon. You said he's all tied up with the Great Bear."

I frowned, then remembered and shrugged. "Whatever."

Afterwards I felt bad. "Later," I muttered.

At morning break Attila started in at me. I knew he would.

"Don't let 'em get to you." He bit into a slab of raisin cake.

"Easy for you," I said. "You try it."

He flicked a sticky raisin away. "If you just—"

"Forget the lecture, right?"

"Yeah, but it's not—"

"I said forget—" I stopped, mid-sentence. The two older guys were coming over.

They didn't walk straight for us. Instead they headed close, passing towards the field. At the last minute the shorter one held up his hand, crooked the pointer finger into a limp curve and gave it a few wobbly flexes. His face grinned behind it.

I was up and after him before I knew I was going to.

Mud flicked off his shoes as he ran. His friend peeled off to the left, guffawing like a donkey but keeping a good eye over his shoulder.

Slick-back was fast, but I was faster. I caught him at the scrum machine and we toppled, bouncing and scraping along the ground, trying to get thumps in before we'd even stopped falling. He landed some hard kicks, but I was all over him, too, with knees, fists and elbows.

The last time I fought anyone I was maybe six, so I don't know how it happened, but some sort of instinct helped me fend off most of his hits and, at the same time, find his weak spots.

We ploughed into the scrum machine, and I landed against iron bars. In the half-second before the guy launched at me again, I registered that it hurt a lot. I braced myself against the machine and managed a couple of good kicks.

He got to his feet and backed off, bent over and huffing, watching me. His arms and legs were smeared with dirt and blood. Hair hung over his face.

Still with an eye on me, he sidled away.

Attila watched, frowning.

Preferred
Subject Matter

Back in class, a few people glanced over.

I suppose I was a bit of a mess. Judging by a clump of stuff near one ear, I had blood in my hair. My face, hands and knees were scraped and stinging. One sock was stuck to my leg with a gluey mixture of mud and grass. All in all, I felt pretty good.

Mrs Ziegler came in late and looked around but obviously didn't notice a thing, and Attila started a "discussion".

ATTILA [SLUMPS IN CHAIR, SPEAKS TO CLASSROOM AT LARGE]: Counting down till we start the non-boring novel.

MRS ZIEGLER [TURNS FROM WHITEBOARD, LOOKS THROUGH HAIR AT WHITEBOARD MARKER, MAKES TWO ATTEMPTS BEFORE CLACKING THE LID ON]: As you persist in saying.

ATTILA [STARES AT CEILING]: Why are the classics so lame? Is it to train us for tooth-rattling boredom? In case we get

locked in a cell with nothing to do except
stare at a wall for decades?

MRS ZIEGLER [LEANS AGAINST WHITEBOARD]:
Patrick. [FOLDS ARMS, CONSIDERS HIM]
I'm aware that you read. In your own way.
Therefore [CLOSES EYES] tell me: what is it
that you most enjoy in . . . in a passage of
text?

ATTILA [FROWNS]: A good story. Obviously.

MRS ZIEGLER [OPENS EYES FOR BRIEFEST SECOND]:
Yes. I expect we've gleaned that much. First
things first—fiction? Or non-fiction?

ATTILA: Fiction, of course. I just said a good
story.

MRS ZIEGLER [NODS]: Yes. Although sometimes
fact is stranger than fiction. [SMILES]
All right. When you read fiction, what, in
particular, do you want to read about?

ATTILA NARROWS EYES, CONSIDERING.

MRS ZIEGLER: Anyone may answer this, in fact.
Your preferred subject matter. Machines?
Zombies? Teenagers? Other aliens? Space
travel?

CLASS GOES QUIET.

CLOCK TICKS IN CORNER.

It never works to wait her out.

CLASS RUSTLES EDGILY.

JOE BRENNER [BREAKS]: Uh—science fiction.

MRS ZIEGLER [SMILE TWITCHES. EYES STILL
    CLOSED]: Thank you, Joe. Anyone else?
SHAUN SMITH: Sharks.
MRS ZIEGLER: Smashing.
ATTILA: Revenge. Battles and revenge. [SMACKS
    DESK] Gory skirmishes. Strung-out, tense
    fire-fights. Devious ambushes and ruthless
    sword fights.
MRS ZIEGLER GIVES EXPLOSIVE, RATTLY LAUGH THAT
    BECOMES LONG AND HELPLESS COUGH. BENDS OVER,
    WHEEZING.

Everyone else started laughing too, mostly at Mrs Ziegler.

Where she'd been leaning, the writing on the whiteboard was
unreadable. Some parts were wiped away completely and others
were smeared, with little lines and squiggles trailing off from the
words where her shirt had rubbed against them. It's always like
that. By the end of the day, her clothes are covered in red or blue
smudges. Sometimes green.

MRS ZIEGLER [STRAIGHTENS, GASPING AND
    STILL MAKING SNORTS OF LAUGHTER. PUSHES
    MARKER-SMUDGED POINTER FINGERS UNDER
    GLASSES TO WIPE EYES. GLASSES JIGGLE
    CROOKEDLY]: Anything else?
ATTILA: Corrupt villains. Bloodthirsty tribes.
CLASS [FLARES INTO UPROAR]:
    —Vampire westerns—
    —Supernatural thrillers—
    —Slash and burn—

—Space opera—

—Biopunk—

—Post-Apocalyptic—

MRS ZIEGLER SQUEEZES EYES SHUT, SHAKES WITH
    LAUGHTER.

ATTILA [BELLOWS]: Which is why we have to
    change the Non-Chosen Novel.

MRS ZIEGLER: What's that? [HAND AT EAR] What
    is it now?

CLASS QUIETENS.

ATTILA: I've got a better Non-Chosen Novel.
    It's got all that stuff. Horror. Werewolves.
    The lot. [PAUSES] At least—it will have.
    [GLANCES AT ME] Soon as I finish writing it.

CLASS [ERUPTS IN PROTEST]: Hey!—I
    voted!—Robo Cougardogs!—You said—The
    spreadsheet—Hockey Were-Mom—

MRS ZIEGLER [BEAMS AT ATTILA]: May I
    say, Patrick, how thrilled I am at
    your aspiration to write a novel.
    However [SCRATCHES HAIR], I would be
    flabbergasted if you were able to finish
    it within the required [LEANS BACKWARDS,
    SQUINTS AT DIARY ON DESK] few days.

ATTILA [WAVES ARMS]: Tut's heard all about it.
    He knows. [POINTS AT ME] It's going like a
    rocket, yes?

ME [SHRUGS]: I'm not . . .

MRS ZIEGLER [REGRETFULLY]: Much as I would
    love to encourage such a super undertaking,

```
     I fear it would take rather longer than the
     time we have at hand.
ATTILA [FROWNS AT ME]: Well?
MRS ZIEGLER: And we certainly won't have
     time—
ATTILA [TO ME, DISBELIEVING]: Tell 'em!
ME [AFTER LONG SILENCE, SHRUGS]: If you say
     so.
```

The lunch bell rang. I pushed everything into my bag and left.

At the far end of the field where the fences barely hold off a jungle of scratchy weeds, I sat on the grass and looked at wind-shorn trees, my lunchbox, and bugs climbing up grass stems.

Nothing really sank in.

I got into an imagined feud with Mike, where I baled him up in a dingy old warehouse and started grilling him: "So ... if you didn't actually see him abandon the guy, how can you be so sure he did?"

In my head Mike said something sly and his eyes slid around, and I yelled, "Ha!" but then I just went back to the beginning of the loop, around and around with no end.

Later a dim thought creaked through that probably I should've waited for Attila at lunchtime. It wasn't strong enough to make me do anything.

I was late back into class and got a stare from Mr Spencer. Attila gave me a funny look too.

Mrs Ziegler

The afternoon passed in a stuffy blur.

On the veranda before last period a kid crept up, quivering, and said Mrs Ziegler wanted to see me after school. Before I could ask what for, he scampered off.

I got there just after the bell.

Mrs Ziegler's room was full of pesky newbs, banging and clattering, dribbling in and out of the door like ball bearings in a puzzle. Mrs Ziegler was up front, wiping the whiteboard with jerky movements.

I stood just inside, wondering if I'd ever been as dozy as this lot. The last few were dawdling, picking up pens or books, putting them down, dithering over bits of paper or just staring around.

The last two left, jabbering, and the door banged behind them. I trailed to the front of the room.

Mrs Ziegler sat in her chair with a sigh.

"Splendid," she said.

She blinked a few times, nodded, and waved for me to sit. "You'll be wondering why I've called you in."

I shrugged, but she was still talking.

"Every now and then," she said, surprisingly, "life is a nasty, mean-spirited cow."

She picked up a black stapler from the left side of her desk, looked at it and put it on top of a messy stack of books on the right side. "And it seems extremely unlikely that it will ever turn the corner. Bounce back. Come up smelling sweet. Pardon the mixed metaphor. Metaphors."

Out on the playing fields someone yelled, "Moroney, ya loser!" and further off a car horn tooted.

"I understand," Mrs Ziegler said, "that there was something of a … skirmish. Earlier today. This morning." She waved a hand towards the playing fields. "Something about a—a scrum machine? I've no idea. No idea. Never mind that. The pertinent fact is, I've called off the hounds."

I had no idea what she was talking about.

"Well," she said, giving her hands a soft, clumsy clap. "I persuaded the more, ah, shall we say … rule-loving factions among the staff to exercise what one might call a touch of leniency." Her face transformed into a look of delight. "I got you off the hook."

"Oh," I said.

The stapler started sliding off the stack of books. Mrs Ziegler snatched it and banged it onto the *Concise Oxford Dictionary*. A staple pinged out the delivery end and landed on the floor.

"I wonder," she said, ignoring the staple, "if I might remind you of our excellent school counsellor. Mr Lowe. A very useful person. For a touch of guidance. A guiding star, you might say—there's an analogy you'll appreciate."

She fiddled with the curled-up corner of a notice on her desk, and glanced up. "Ah. I see the suggestion lacks appeal."

"Um," I said. I was thinking of the counsellor, and how much use he'd been.

"I mention it only as a possibility," said Mrs Ziegler. "No offence, if you prefer to pass."

I shuffled in the chair. "Yeah. I think I might—y'know—give it a miss. Thanks, though."

She gave a birdy twitch and nodded. "Not at all." She beamed, and flapped a hand at me to go.

Bizarrely, Attila was waiting.

He fell into step, and we went out the gate and up towards the war memorial.

Attila kicked a stone at the gutter. It bounced off the edge of the pavement and into the road. I kept walking.

He kicked another couple, in quick succession. I kept walking.

Head down, he scuffed a whole scree of stones towards the gutter and said, "It's getting annoying."

"What is?" I said automatically.

He didn't answer. I looked over.

"The sulks." He kicked another stone. "You're obsessed."

I stared at him, enraged but still walking.

He looked stubborn. "You could've backed me up. The Non-Chosen Novel."

"Oh, I get it." I booted a couple of stones myself. "Well, maybe I would've, if you hadn't preached a sermon at me."

He walked faster. "You don't have to prove anything."

I stopped. "What's that mean?"

He turned and came back a couple of steps. His usual flippant grin was a long way off. "You don't have to prove your dad was a good climber. Or a good adventurer. Or a good *dad*. Any of that crap." He shoved his head forward. "You should know if he was or wasn't. You should know that stuff. Yes?" He jerked his bag further up his shoulder. "You don't have to prove it to those idiots. Forget them. They're jerks."

There was a silence.

"Well," I yelled suddenly. "That's the whole thing." My hands, squeezed into clumps at my sides, felt oversized and hot. "Isn't it?" I wasn't in control of my mouth. "I don't know it. Can't you see that? I don't know. So—" I leaned into his goggling face and jabbed a finger at his shirt— "how the hell would I prove it to someone else?"

Tom the Climber

That was a bolt from the blue.

It was only a few hours earlier I was scheming to get to the truth—that Dad didn't abandon the client.

The search engine pondered, and, looking out the window, I did too. The screen loaded and I scrolled through.

Bootzwench: Yeah, obviously above 8000m all bets are off. Your body's basically shutting down, & the longer you're up there the worse it gets. So - - - YOU try telling someone who can barely breathe to stop and help some other poor bastard. It's not gonna happen.

GregO93: I have been following this thread, and I must come in here. I speak from experience. When people with only moderate skills believe they can climb the highest peaks in the world, they become highly dangerous, both to themselves and others.

Bootzwench: Oh so GregO93, you reckon some guy who's struggling, he shouldn't be on the mountain? Because he's gonna turn into a problem for someone? What right have you or anyone got to tell him he can or can't go up there?

That thing about people turning into a problem—Dad always said it. Climbers who couldn't cope shouldn't be up there. It reminded me of Tom, who came to our place to ask about the next expedition.

He had that climber look. Not that they're all the same, or even mostly. But a lot have a wiry, gristly appearance. Dad got talking to him, and their voices filtered through the sunroom wall, droning in a distorted way about the weather and who'd climbed what lately and what the newest equipment was like.

They went out on the veranda, and Dad went back to checking climbing gear by my window. He finished the carabiners and started running a rope through his hands, feeling for faults. "From what you're saying, you've been to six-five or seven. Nothing over eight."

Eight thousand metres and up, the Death Zone.

Tom started talking, but Dad interrupted. "It wouldn't be a problem, if you'd done the last five, six seasons. Good challenging stuff." He kept feeding the rope through his hands. "It's better if you keep building on it. Get some higher peaks under your belt."

Tom started in again, but Dad cut over him. "Aconcagua, say. McKinley. Maybe a couple of the Mexican ones."

The rope kept moving, sliding through Dad's hands and slapping quietly against the table, but Tom had gone silent. Dad didn't even notice.

"Anyone who goes has to be high-functioning at the upper altitudes. Excellent crampon technique on snow and ice. Plenty of experience with crevasse rescues and glaciers." He brandished the rope. "Rope ascending. Rappelling. And at least five years of high-altitude stuff, back-to-back seasons. Also—" he paused— "you have to really, really want the summit."

"My skills are good," said Tom. "And I bloody well do want—"

"No," Dad interrupted again. "I won't take the risk."

I remember heating up with embarrassment, but Dad carried on. "It's not just you who's affected. Obviously."

Tom got into a temper and started shouting, about Dad being arrogant and judging him too quickly. Dad told him to leave and he went, slamming the front door. A few months later I heard Dad telling Mum that Tom had got to the summit with another company. He sounded annoyed.

Good old Tom, I thought.

I sighed, remembering how riled-up I'd got with Attila, and stared again at the forum comments. Bootzwench was well into it, ranting about free will and human rights. Someone else started in, saying she should calm down and stop being so bossy.

Another time, I remembered, one of the climbing guys had been talking about a rope he'd ordered. It was a bit cheaper than usual, he said, but the safety rating was almost as good.

"Come on," said Dad. "When you need the extra, you *need* it."

The guy started saying something else, but Dad cut him off. "Don't do it. Anyone who scrimps on safety's a fool."

Later, when everyone had gone, Mum said, "Couldn't you be more tactful?" She got irritated other times too, when they had friends over and Dad said something dogmatic. He'd never be budged, either. "Your precious principles," Mum would say afterwards. "Can't you lighten up?"

The phone rang.

No one answered.

I wouldn't be rushing out there. Mum could do it for once.

Then Fen crashed out his door. He never answers the phone. His high voice said, "Hello?"

"Yes," he said.

"Yes," again.

Then, a bit panicky, "I don't know."

When I got there he was staring at the receiver, looking fretful.

"Here," I muttered.

"She wants Mum."

"Who is it?"

He shoved the phone at me.

"Hello?"

"Oh," said Celia's voice. "I'm sorry. Is that—who is that, please?"

"It's Tuttle. Um, Duncan."

"Oh." She sounded relieved. "Hello. It's Celia Guinn. Could I speak with your mum, please?" She paused. "Fen didn't seem to know where she is."

I didn't know either. I pictured her in the chair, sleeping.

Which was none of Celia's business.

Oh. Maybe it was.

"She's here. Putting out the washing. Or vacuuming."

"Oh." She sounded flustered. "I was ringing about our meeting this afternoon."

"Meeting?"

"I was just telling Fen. I'm so sorry, but I'm running late. Could I come a little later, would it still work? Could you ask Rose?"

"She'll be here. What time?"

"Well—" Something rustled and her voice went muffled, then came back. "Can we say ... six-twenty?"

"Yeah."

"It's late, sorry—I hope it won't clash with your dinner. You're sure it'll suit your mum?"

"Yes."

Fen had disappeared into his room.

"Lovely," said Celia. "I'll see you all later, thanks very—"

"Um," I said.

Nothing happened, and I thought she must have hung up. Then she said, "Yes?"

"Oh. Just—what's it about?"

There was a silence. "Well. It's really just seeing how you're all getting on." More rustling. "I'm just off to a meeting. And then—" her voice went chirpy and cheerful— "I'll come and see you all. And we'll talk things through."

"Okay," I said.

"It's nothing to be concerned about. All right?"

"All right," I said.

The Instinct

Mum was in the bedroom chair.

"Social Services," I said from the doorway. "She's running late. What's going on?"

"She rang earlier. She didn't say. Tut?"

"Yeah?"

She sank lower in the chair. "What if they take you away?"

Things slowed down.

Not so long ago, when Mum barely talked, I'd have liked the sound of pretty much anything she had to say. I didn't like this. I didn't want to hear it. Jeez, she was crying.

"I haven't been coping. Maybe they think you need a man around." She sniffed. "Social Services."

Then I heard a sound behind me and turned, and there was Fen standing goggle-eyed in the hallway. He was backed into the plant by the window, a couple of dry stems tangled in his hair.

In a few seconds Mum was kneeling in front of him.

He'd put on a savage scowl, but he was close to bawling. He pulled further into the plant. "Why'd you let him go?"

"Who? Let who go?"

"Dad," he shouted. Tears dripped down his face, but he didn't care or hadn't noticed. "You should've kept him here! It's your fault! If you'd kept him here—" He whacked the plant, making it crackle. "I wish you'd died instead!"

He shoved past and ran down the hallway.

His bedroom door banged.

Neither of us said anything for a while.

It was a shock hearing him say it. But it wasn't like I could take the moral high ground. Once or twice when things got really bleak, I'd thought the same thing.

Mum was still kneeling by the plant. She scratched at a piece of fluff on the carpet and muttered, "Funny."

"What is?" Not that she was laughing. She looked a lot like Fen before he took off. Enraged, but on the brink of crying. And sickly.

"I hounded him."

I could barely hear her mumbling. "What?" I said louder. "You hounded Fen?"

"Jamie. Before he left for Everest, that last morning. We argued."

I didn't move.

She was still fiddling with the bit of fluff. Absentmindedly she picked it up. "I put huge pressure on him. Not to take chances on the mountain. 'No heroic moments,' I said. 'No risking your life.'"

The crying part was starting to win, I could see.

"That's not all. I said that if he did—you know, take risks—he was as good as abandoning his family." She got louder. "I made it nice and definite. So he'd have no doubt."

"But—I don't get it."

Her glare turned impatient. It was better, somehow.

"He had the instinct. He was a natural. Left to himself, of course he'd have saved Stephen. And himself. But," she raised the fingers with the fluff and shook them, like a teacher driving home a point, "when I put so much pressure on him, I messed up his instinct.

"So you see, it's my fault he abandoned Stephen Pritcher on the mountain. And my fault he died."

Castor & Pollux

I saw a clip of a boxer once who was groggy from too many hits. It was gruesome. He couldn't see the next punch coming, so he kept getting clobbered, over and over.

I understood how he must have felt. Too much was going on.

I left Mum where she was. I didn't feel great about that, but I had to check on Fen.

Something inside his bedroom was making a regular hollow clunking. I knocked. There was no reply. I went in anyway.

He was on the edge of the lower bunk, banging his feet against the plastic boxes under the bed and turning something around in his hands.

"All right?" I said.

He watched the thing in his hands go round.

"We'll sort it out," I said. "Y'know. Stick together."

Impressive, I know. Emotional support is my speciality.

It was a belay clip he was holding. I hadn't seen one for a long time. Mum put all the climbing stuff away months ago.

I leaned against his green chest of drawers. Elmo's drawer was open, but there was no sign of Elmo himself.

"Hey. Have I told you about Castor and Pollux?"

He didn't look up.

"Brothers," I said. "Well—half-brothers. One mortal, one immortal." I got a couple of pencils off his desk, absently put them in chopsticks mode, and made pincer movements. "They knew the mortal one would die eventually, and they didn't want to get split up. So they asked Zeus to arrange it so they could stay together forever."

Fen started clicking the carabiner loudly open and closed. His feet were still going.

"You might think," I said over the noise, "the decent thing would be for Zeus to say, 'Yeah, okay, I'll give you both immortality. Then you can stick together.' But no." I paused for comic effect. "Instead, he shoved them both up in the sky."

Fen used to love the Zeus punchline. Not this time. One of his feet was banging harder than the other.

"They were the patron saints of sailors. Castor and Pollux."

He didn't seem to be listening. Bang bang, bang bang.

"Patron saints of sailors and boats."

With a huge bound, he leapt off the bed. "Leave me alone!"

I was so surprised I dropped the pencils. They clattered onto the floor. "Why d'you always hang around?" he yelled. "Asking how I am?"

I stared. I admit I was shocked.

"I'm not a baby!" His eyes looked like bursting out. He rocked back and bumped into the bed.

By then I was getting over the surprise. "What the hell?"

One of his flailing arms hit the stack of library books on his desk. The top one slipped off the pile and fell.

He kicked out as it went, but missed.

With a wild hook of both hands, he shoved the whole lot sideways off the desk. They crashed onto the floor. He straightened and shrieked, "And why do you have to tell stupid *stories* all the time?"

Out in the hallway Celia's voice said, "Hello? Is everything all right? I let myself in."

Elmo

I closed Fen's door gently behind me.

Muttering drifted out of the living room. First Celia, then Mum. Then Celia.

In my own room I picked up the computer and went out again.

It was getting dark, with a few stripes of yellow cloud across the west. The shed doorknob rattled as always. The glasshouse windows were half-opaque with dust and blotches, but bits of evening light came through. I shoved the computer onto the potting table.

What a dazzling, spectacular stuff-up.

There I was, going along thinking, Yeah, well, things aren't great, but at least I'm helping Fen. Making sure he eats. Getting him to school. Washing his clothes. At least something's working. He's got his big brother looking after him, bucking him up.

I sat for a long time on an upside-down bucket while the light got fainter. At one point I heard the front door open. Voices murmured. Someone, Celia by the dim shape through the windows, tapped away down the path. The front door closed and everything went quiet.

I wanted to know what she'd been saying to Mum. And what she thought she was doing, poking her nose in here again.

That little silence at the other end of the phone, when I'd asked what the meeting was about. That bugged me. And when she said, "It's nothing to be concerned about. All right?" Right. Who'd she gone to see before she came to our place? A foster family?

The computer sat on the potting table, looking innocent.

It was pointless checking again. The forums weren't about to offer up a miraculous reason why James Theodorus did what he did. A blow-by-blow account, say, of what happened on the mountain, from someone's brother-in-law's cousin who was right on the spot right at the time, with a little note at the end: "Hell, it was Stephen's dying wish. He begged Jamie to go looking for someone else. That's why it happened."

So. No happy endings on the forums. It'd be more useful— probably more fun—sandpapering my eyes.

The front door opened again. Mum called. She went out on the veranda and called again. She sounded upset. After a while she went back in.

I got up and shuffled around in the dry planty smell, feeling like an old man. A couple of birds chirped outside. The house was silent. A light went on at the back—the living room, maybe, or the kitchen. Now and then a whiff came through from the shed, of timber or paint.

Down on the floor by the shed doorstep, an old wooden crate was stuffed up against the wall. Inside was a scrap of something red. I squatted in front for a better look.

The crate was full of Dad's beer-making things. Incredible— something Mum had missed in her rabid clear-out. One of the bottles even had a label, wrinkled and faded, with tall old-fashioned lettering: *Comet Brew*. I had a feeling Mum had designed it. A blue and green rocket blasted off to the right, and across the top was a comet with a long tail of beer froth.

An old clay pot half covered the bit of red I'd seen. When I pulled it away, there was Fen's Elmo, flopped over and mangled. His red fur was stuck flat with dust, and he was essentially dismembered—his arms and legs ripped away from his body and hanging by threads. When I held him up in the blue computer light, they dangled.

It didn't seem right to put him back where I'd found him, stuck down in the dust, but it also seemed wrong to take him inside. I propped him on an old paint tin in the middle of the shed where he'd be obvious if anyone went looking, sitting up as much as he could in his broken state.

I started gaming.

And lost every time. Spectacularly.

My stomach gurgled and whined, but I kept going. The glass-house got dark. I lowered the screen brightness and turned the computer away from the house.

I should have thought of luck-based games sooner. I smacked and walloped the keys, bashed the spacebar, and kicked the rickety legs of the potting table. Hours went by. I stopped being hungry. My scores improved—I was on a roll. 8.50 p.m., 9.34. Whenever I won, I belted the screen and hunched over for another go. When I lost, I just belted the screen. Smack, for the reporter. Smack, for Boyd. One or two for the idiot-mobile. A smack for Slick-back, and another for all the hecklers at school. An extra good crack for the forum commenters and their big opinions.

11.13.

11.58.

The screen turned into smudges suddenly. It was all a bit much. Bed, and sleep, seemed good places to be.

Outside I stood noticing the quiet. The sky was mostly clear, with a few drab clouds, and there was a waiting feel. I woke up a little with the cold.

The kitchen clock said 12.18 a.m. (And, zap: 6.03 p.m. Nepal Standard Time.) Mum's voice drifted out of the living room, stopping and starting in phone-speak. This time of night, it must be Aunty Sally.

I went for the fridge on sock steps.

Mum had gone quiet.

I stopped, listening.

Round the corner she sniffed. Then she said, "How could they take them away?"

My hand was still stretched out for the fridge door.

"How could they?" she said, louder. My arm hung in the air. "When we've been through so much?"

I left the milk and went to my room.

On the Road

We'd get a bus to Uncle Neal's. He'd hide us. If Social Services came looking, we'd sneak into the pigpen or the chicken shed, or some other place they'd never think of. Up a haystack. Down a well. When everyone stopped searching, we'd move to a different country.

It'd be fine.

What a lousy, sneaky schemer Celia had turned out to be. All the time she was acting so nice, flashing her caring smile, she was actually one of those power-hungry, two-faced dictators pulling everyone's strings. What gave her the right to play high-and-mighty with our lives?

Things weren't ideal, maybe. But we were eating enough. Generally. Getting to school, mostly on time. Staying clean.

The memory of Fen's pee-soaked trousers slunk in. What a moron I was. We weren't coping. And if we left, Uncle Neal's would be one of the first places they'd look.

It'd have to be just me and Fen, on the road.

I'd tell him it was an adventure. Like in his books. He'd be right into that. Especially if I told him there'd be trains.

I looked around my room again, and I admit I got a bit pathetic and desperate, just for a minute.

Boyd's airhorn started up, maybe a block away, blaring Dixie down the street. A few seconds later his car drift-slid, rubber shrieking, into the drive next door.

Then for a while it was the Boyd & Derek Show—thumping stereo, whooping and yahooing inside the car, revving in sync with the music, more whooping, and on and on.

Finally they stalled the engine and got out.

They kept up the yelling, though, back and forth over the car. I saw them out the window, black ant-figures hopping.

Derek got on his scooter and buzzed off. Boyd went inside and slammed the door.

I was so angry I could barely breathe. My hands were shaking like in a movie. Even though I couldn't have put two words together, it felt like I followed a memorized drill.

Old polyprop gloves on. Chisel from toolbox. Window and curtains open for a quick return.

All quiet in the house. Same for street.

Then shoes on, out the window, across the veranda, under the trees with the chisel held out in front, over the fence and thud onto the ground, then up close to the ticking, creaking car.

The metalwork had little blobs of dew, and orange reflections glinted on the roof. The dark had stripped the machine of its up-yours red, but it was still just as cocky. I got on my knees beside a tyre and jabbed hard with the chisel.

The thump went up my arms, but the hissing I expected didn't happen. I jiggled the tool, yanked it out and shoved it in harder.

It went further this time, so I pushed, twisting the blade.

I heard a first little hiss.

It got louder. I rocked the handle back and forth.

The tyre gasped, flopped, and settled gently onto the concrete, shushing out an oily rubber smell.

If anything, I was calmer than before. The rage was parked, waiting in the background. I learned the best spot to jab. It was hard work. Sweat stung in my eyes. By the third one I was a pro: stab, rock, rock some more and wait for the *give*, pull back to control the hiss, let the air out gently, feel the pressure fall, open the gash more.

Doing the fourth one I glanced around and saw a little pile of bricks at the edge of the lawn. Six or eight of them, tilting over each other in the crispy grass. My next trick.

First, I put a good deep set of scratches along the side panels, because that's quiet.

Then I hurled a brick at the driver's window.

It felt very good.

But it was unbelievably loud. Glass went everywhere, into the car and out, and the next second it was grating and crunching under my feet. I looked at the brick, resting crooked on the passenger's seat, and noticed my mouth was stretched out in a big grin.

But there wasn't time to think about it, because lights were coming on everywhere.

I collected the chisel on the way out.

In & Out

In my room I went round and round, then dropped onto the bed.

Outside, people ran and shouted. Doors banged. Beams of light flicked across the trees and onto the street.

Mum said something in the hallway.

My sneakers snagged on the duvet, but I got the thing over my head and flopped down, holding my breath.

The light changed with the door opening.

Mum came in. Her footsteps went across to the window. Then she creaked back to my bed and whispered, "You awake?" and touched my shoulder. I didn't move.

She went away and closed the door.

I heard a faint siren. Getting closer, fast. And louder, fast. I pulled the duvet off my face. It was insanely loud. And there were flashing lights. Car doors banged, and more torchlight flickered.

The siren stopped with a winding-down blurt and an odd pocket of quiet afterwards. The flashing lights kept going. The police car radio made belchy static noises, and there were confident voices and scuffling and rattling.

They stayed thirty-nine minutes. Partway through, they turned off the flashing lights.

It's a funny thing with lights like that. They get into a pattern, a sort of rippling that flows and repeats in rhythms, and it's only when they stop that you realize you were beating along in your head the whole time.

A car started up.

There was more talking—loud, "going now" talking—and more scratchy radio burps. A car door closed. An engine revved, then faded away down the street.

After that it was just faint muttering, rattles, a bit of scraping on concrete—a shovel, maybe—and clinking glass and a few muted grunts.

Then quiet.

I went back to circling the floor.

My mind jumped around. For a second I'd go back to the shushing rubber, or the curls of paint coming off the chisel, or the glass crunching under my sneaker. Then I'd flick away. And every five seconds I peered around the edge of the curtain.

I wanted to be out.

But Boyd might be waiting—hidden away, hoping the vandal would come back for another go.

I crept down the hallway, then into the living room, keeping an ear out for Mum. The outside door stuck and creaked, then I was out and crouched on the veranda. I slithered across the boards and dropped onto grass. The light angling across from Boyd's place followed me, like in one of those prison movies—I expected a commando shout, or the clatter of boots on the fence.

Three seconds later I was rocketing up the treehouse planks.

Inside the hut, a few buckets and tools made shimmery shapes on the shelves. The hammock was a pale blur in the corner. I backed out, scaled the handrail, and climbed.

The bark had knobbly bits to grip and deep crooked grooves for toeholds. From memory, the first part was a long way up with nowhere to rest. Good.

Celia had the perfect excuse now.

I heaved myself over a branch, sniffing, and my nose dripped stuff on the branches below.

The treehouse roof was already a long way down, and hard to see under a layer of old leaves. The wind gusted. Above, there wasn't much except leafy branches and clouds and occasional shreds of sky. The outer twigs, easiest to see against the sky, were bent in crazy shapes. Here and there moonlight spotted the trunk, showing humps and black knotholes on the bigger branches.

A wide view of the city appeared, way below. A few lights showed at the girls' college in Thorndon. College seemed a long time ago. I didn't fancy the thought of going back. Facing up to Attila, for a start. That'd be fun.

And then sitting in class, or in a lab or assembly, waiting, knowing the police were figuring out clues. Closing in, minute by minute. Slapping scribbled Post-It notes on whiteboards and staring squint-eyed at them. Putting it all together.

On the other hand, maybe I wouldn't be going back to college. Maybe Social Services would make it quick and easy, and move us straight away.

New suburb, new parents, new school.

The tree swayed and I kept going.

Saint Erasmus

These branches were thinner, with more air between them. Some of the clouds were clearing away. Craning, I got a glimpse of Sirius—so Canis Major, the Great Dog, was galloping along up there. Its prey, Lepus the Hare, was behind clouds.

When Social Services came I'd be calm and reasonable.

"We're on the road to recovery," I'd say. "Just give us a chance."

I pictured everyone gathered in the living room. Celia. Mum and Fen. Probably a couple of guys in white overalls (only a guess—who knows what they wear to march people away?). And me, telling them.

It was only fair to have a chance to sort things out. Celia could put that in her blue and brown file.

Below, the city glittered. I knew what would really happen.

Social Services would say, "I'm sorry, but it's time to go."

Like Zeus, basically: This is how it's gonna be. Get used to it.

I thought about all the counsellors and Social Services people out there in their offices with their blue and brown folders, deciding the fates of us poor suckers. It's a pretty poor state of affairs, when everyone else gets to decide what happens to you.

Overhead, a pale Southern Cross showed up behind wispy clouds. Castor and Pollux appeared too, but the moonlight faded them. For a second or two it was exhilarating, being at the top of a tree in the middle of the night with black sky, pale stars and gusts of wind. Like being at the tip of a ship's mast. The tree moved in a gust and I grabbed on, muttering, "Ahoy."

In thunderstorms now and then, the pointy part of a ship's mast gets a freaky blue light around it called St Elmo's Fire. It's something to do with electrical fields and voltage differences, and it's named after St Elmo, a.k.a. St Erasmus, the patron saint of sailors. Which is confusing, when you consider that Castor and Pollux are also supposed to be the protectors of sailors and boats.

A few more stars appeared. I looked up at them in the black, and pretty soon I got that feeling of nothingness—of everything vast and empty.

Usually it's a good kind of nothingness. Not so much this time. I sat there cooling off, and clouds eddied round, and it hit me how alone I was—and how scared.

And what I'd done.

Wrecking the idiot-mobile was just the latest in a string of genius ideas. But it was the one that demonstrated best how much like Dad I was. Instead of telling Boyd to shove his car where it hurt, I'd done the gutless thing and trashed it in the dark.

There was no getting around it. I was a chip off the old block—arrogant, tactless and full of big opinions. And a coward. When something really mattered, I got it spectacularly wrong.

In a storm, seeing St Elmo's Fire is supposed to be good luck.

Though depending on who you're talking to, it can also mean very, very bad luck.

Sneaking

Leaves shifted. But not with the wind. I looked down past my sneaker, which was wedged in a gap.

Below, Fen was looking for a foothold.

"What the hell?"

He was mostly just a face blob with dark eye blobs. His voice drifted up in the dark. "I came to find you."

"Get down. What're you thinking? You'll fall."

"I saw you go," he said. "I followed you."

"Have you been sneaking around?"

"Not sneaking."

I had to ask. "Where'd you follow me?"

He answered slowly, as if to a moron. "Up the tree."

"Yeah? When I thought you were sick of the lame stories."

He didn't answer that. "Why did you come up here?"

"None of your business." My foot hurt. I twisted it free. "We're going down now."

He didn't move. Another gust pushed the tree. I looked down, and a twinge of dizziness made me close my eyes.

Something tapped my foot. "Move. I want to come up."

I breathed carefully out. "No. It's not safe."

"I want to come up," said Fen, louder.

If he would just shut up. "Get off, you little—"

He sucked in an indignant breath, grabbed my sneaker and pushed hard. "Move this foot."

I opened my eyes in surprise.

Vertigo sailed in, scooping a hole in my guts. I clutched with fingernails and knees. Under the noise in my head, Fen's voice insisted. "Move your foot."

"Can't."

"Why not?" he said, and shoved again. Everything lurched.

"Don't!"

I could hear my own panic.

His hand went away.

He said in a confounded voice, "Are you scared?"

Toliman & Hadar

The universe looped the loop.

It wasn't a good feeling. Not good at all.

"It's vertigo." It came out in a silly bleat. I shut my eyes, but the whirling wouldn't stop. "Interesting thing," I whispered. Any distraction. "About the Pointers."

Fen didn't answer.

"Y'know Alpha Centauri's one of them. And Beta Centauri. They look like stars."

Silence.

I waited out more giddiness. "Everyone *calls* them stars."

He was breathing through his mouth.

"But they're not. They're multiple stars." I could practically hear him frowning. "Close together," I said. "Too close to see apart." Something rustled, and my innards swooped again. "Keep still."

The noise subsided.

"They've got other names," I said.

Still no answer.

"Alpha Centauri is Rigil Kentaurus. Or Rigil Kent. Sometimes Toliman."

Something touched my shoe. "There's a place for your foot," said Fen. "Down here." He squeezed. "Just bring it here."

"No," I said. "See, Toliman comes from Arabic. It means 'the ostriches'. I dunno exactly why ostriches, but they'll have had their reasons. And Beta—"

"Try," said Fen. "It's not far." He squeezed again.

"—Beta Centauri, it's got other names, Hadar and Agena. But I don't know where they're from."

My fingers had taken on the shape of the branch. "Alpha Centauri's the closest star system to us."

"Try," said Fen.

The dizziness seemed maybe a fraction less. I couldn't be sure. I waited, breathed, and cracked an eye open. Everything was darker than I remembered. And colder.

"It's not far," Fen said.

I kept my eyes fixed on the tree trunk and moved my foot a tiny amount. "Alpha Centauri's the third brightest star."

Fen pressed again, slightly harder. I moved the same amount. "A bit more," he said.

"Beta Centauri's the eleventh brightest."

"Just here."

"The Pointers mark the front legs of Centaurus, the centaur constellation."

"Come on," said Fen. His hand tugged.

I shuffled forward, still clutching on.

My butt was almost off the branch when I started sliding.

I panicked, and floundered with both feet flailing. My arms slipped and scraped around the branch.

Fen's hand grabbed my leg and pushed, and my reaching foot hit something and curved around it.

The perch held. "There," said Fen.

I kept still, just breathing.

Fen had gone lower. He nudged my leg. "Bring this one."

I inched the shoe sideways. "Centaurus is named after Chiron. A centaur in the Greek myths. He taught all the heroes. Herakles, Achilles, Jason. All those ones. Even Asclepius—remember him, the guy who brought people back from the dead?"

Hugging the branch until the last second, I slid down the bark, then moved one hand to a new hold. And the other.

We were still a long way up.

"More," he said. I squeezed between two branches, slid down onto a bigger one and hung my leg over. A twig rasped my ankle. Hands nudged my foot onto a branch.

"There," said Fen.

I tested the hold. It felt solid.

I still felt sick. But every lower branch helped.

Now and then, moonlight speckled our faces and arms. I got random glimpses of Fen, concentrating, or nodding or blinking, or looking for the next foothold.

The bark was rougher under my hands.

"Hey!" yelped Fen. "A shooting star! Did you *see* it?"

"No. Shut up. Keep still."

The roof of the treehouse showed up murkily below. Night things shifted and creaked. We kept going.

Fen balanced on the treehouse railing.

I eased down beside him, sighed, and sat. My bones slumped and drifted into the damp timber. I might, I thought slowly, stay forever. Right here.

The night-time rustlings and shufflings gradually got louder and closer. The air felt colder around my face.

"Thanks," I said.

I looked sideways. Fen was messing with a twig.

"Y'know," I said. "Getting me down."

He showed a smudge of white teeth. "It's okay."

It sounded like he might add something, but he didn't. "What?" I said.

I swear I saw a couple of the old dimples make darker spots on his cheeks. He shrugged, and rolled his head. "Just ... I don't *really* hate the stories."

I scratched my neck and said, "Good," and that was that.

Saturn in Your Bathroom

Fen looked up, past the bulk of the tree. "Which one is it again? Closest to us?"

I sighed. "Don't you listen to a thing I bore you senseless with?"

He snorted, then hiccupped.

"The single star closest to our solar system," I intoned, "is Alpha Centauri C. Also known as Proxima Centauri." The Pointers and Southern Cross glinted. The sky around them was a rich, dark black. "Course, it's invisible to the naked eye."

Fen sucked in a gleeful gasp. "You said *naked*."

"Grow up."

He landed off the railing with a thud and said, "I remember when Dad fixed the solar system."

I stopped, ready to jump. "You what?"

"The solar system. When you put it in the tree."

"Uh ... still not with you."

He frowned. "The solar system."

Suddenly I remembered. "The kitset."

"You would have left it there," he said, mildly accusing. "It'd still be there.'

164

I followed him into the treehouse.

It took him a couple of goes, but he wrangled himself into the hammock and settled with a long sigh. A gust of wind moved things around outside and his voice came out of the dark, faded and sleepy. "I watched him fix it. After."

I stood in the doorway, remembering. Fen wouldn't have known, but I'd watched the fixing, too. In a sulk, from behind my bedroom curtain.

He said, even sleepier, "Filled up the holes."

I'd flung the whole kit out my window in a gluey-fingered rage. It landed in the spikiest shrub in the garden, and the nylon lines turned instantly—*instantly*, it wasn't physically even possible— into a snarly horror show.

Fen said, quite slowly, "And put white on them."

Jupiter and Neptune, in particular, had come off badly.

Fen's breathing was a lot slower. I went over.

He was asleep like a baby. His hood was curled around his face, making him look almost angelic. Only in that light, of course.

I thought for a while. Then, warily, I went back out and climbed the handrail and up to the treehouse roof.

The edges of the iron were sharp, but the leaves and twigs on top were soft, even warm. I eased out onto my back and looked up.

Low cloud was drifting in. It looked like rain.

A morepork hooted a long way off. I listened to the tree, and thought about the solar-system kit. The blue and white Earth. Red Mars. Dad's fingers tying the nylon lines. My painstakingly daubed spot on Jupiter. The rings of Saturn. Saturn had seemed huge, even while it was just a little styrofoam ball in my hand.

Dad taught me a couple of knots he said would never slip, and we put the whole thing up that night in the middle of my ceiling.

When I went to bed I left the door open, so the hallway light would show the dangling, slowly bobbing worlds.

Of course, if we'd wanted the distances to be to scale, Jupiter would have had to be a few blocks from our place. That would've been something—walking around with a map, knocking on a random stranger's door and saying, "Excuse me, would you mind putting Saturn in your bathroom? My calculations show ..."

The leaves on the treehouse roof had a sharpish smell, but it wasn't bad. Drizzle started falling quietly and straight down. A snore came up from Fen below. I held a hand over my face and looked between my fingers, and while everything dripped I lay in the quiet damp and thought about Dad.

His fast way of moving, and his crazy hair, and his irritable need sometimes to get out and climb a rock. His lame sayings, like "Make it so" and "Good thinking, Ninety-Nine". The climbing-wall sessions. The beer brewing and the times in the sunroom. Packing up his gear for a mountain. Acting the Greek philosopher. The falling-out with Tom the client. Even his arguments with Mum.

I took my hand away and let the rain fall on my face, and lay there remembering and sniffing, and the rain mixed up with maybe a couple of tears and slid down cold around my ears, but it didn't matter.

Maybe because of the solar-system kit, I started thinking again about that space probe, Pioneer 11.

It's out there, zillions of kilometres away and zooming further every second, and at the same time—all the time—it's stashing bits and bytes of data, never stopping. But it can't send the data home. It doesn't have the power any more.

Meanwhile, Dad can't tell anyone what he knows, either.

But, bizarrely, it turns out I don't need to know.

It's a funny thing. After a while (a long while, even), the things you thought you could never cope with, you can. Somehow, after all the time you spend mulling them over—including when you didn't even know you were mulling—finally you just think, Yeah, I guess. I guess it's like that.

And you think, Yeah, actually I can manage it like that.

It was getting lighter.

A bird somewhere did a sleepy chirp.

The rain was only a few specks now, barely enough to notice.

Around about then, I remembered the counsellor and how he'd suggested writing Dad a letter. I'd never heard anything so moronic. And I certainly won't be doing it.

But if, just for example, I was going to maybe *say* something to Dad—well. It'd be this:

It's fine. It really is.

I don't know if you got it right, that last time.

But mostly you did.

No one gets it right all the time.

Back to Earth

Down below, the living-room door did its shuddery bang. Mum's voice shrieked, "Tuttle? *Fen*? *Tuttle*! Where are you?"

"Here," I said.

Silence.

"Up here," I said. "The treehouse."

Another silence. Her footsteps stamped across the veranda, down the steps and onto the lawn. From directly below she yelled, "Fen. Where's Fen?"

"He's here." I shuffled to the roof edge and dangled a leg over, swinging it around for the handrail. "Gone into orbit by now."

"What are you doing?" Mum shouted. "I've been out of my mind with worry—rushing around the house—"

My toe found the rail, and I eased over the edge.

"—on the verge of ringing the police." She was yelling louder, if anything. "Freaking out—do you realize it's five in the morning—just what is going on here?"

Crouched on the handrail, I could see her below, jigging from foot to foot. "Where's Fen? Where is he?"

Fen bumbled through the treehouse doorway. "Mum?"

"Love." She reached her arms up. "Come down." She sighed. "Both of you. Get down here. Now."

Fen went first, surprisingly fast for someone who'd just woken up, but I took my time. When I stepped off the bottom plank and turned, Mum was by the trunk, hugging Fen and glaring over his head at me with a mix of rage and relief.

"D'you think there's not enough drama in our lives?" she said. "Is that it?"

If she only knew. Jeez.

She grabbed at me, staggering with Fen stuck to her like a limpet, and pulled so I had to join the group hug. It was painfully tight, but I didn't mind too much.

Though it did make me think again about the fostering, which I did mind.

Then Mum did a big sniff and got business-like.

"Fen. Bed."

Over his immediate bleat of complaint she said louder, "Straight to bed. No discussion." She paused, and said in what I thought was a cunning tone, "Bed, and no school."

That shut him up. He gave me a faint, possibly conspiratorial grin. Mum headed back to the house, pushing him ahead of her. "And you," she said over her shoulder. "Shower. You're soaked. Then we will talk."

Uh oh. This was like old times. She was really getting into the parenting now.

"Wait," said Fen. "Wait."

He pulled away and bolted for the corner of the house.

"Fen! Get back here! What the—Fen!"

"I'll be back!" he yelled, and scuttled away around the side of the house. "Wait!" came again, quieter.

Mum turned with a disbelieving stare. I held up my hands. "Don't look at me."

There was a noise—the shed door?—and distant scuffling. Something banged again. Steps started back, pounded closer, and Fen reappeared at the corner of the house.

He came closer and held out the jumble in his arms.

"Will you fix him?"

I took the grimy bundle of Elmo. "Yeah."

I did have a shower, just to get warm. Then I put on dry clothes and sat at my desk and wrote some things. Mum and Fen were mumbling next door.

A few minutes later I tiptoed down the hallway and into the kitchen, picking up my sneakers on the way.

It wasn't a great feeling, putting the note on the kitchen bench. Other than that, I was still pretty calm.

Mum, sorry but I need to go somewhere. I'll come back after. We can talk then if you want. T.

Outside, the rain had drifted off. It was still dark enough to show a few stars.

Rights & Mints

I got to the police station just after six and took up a position across the road so I'd see when it opened. A few seconds later some guy came out the doors, clattered down the steps and went off whistling down Victoria Street.

Peculiar.

But then I had a eureka moment. Hadn't someone at school said the central station never closed?

I crossed over and started up the steps.

My legs wouldn't operate at normal speed. I couldn't hurry them up. At this rate, it'd take all morning to get to the top.

Boy, 14, completes slowest ascent in history.

It's a pretty ordinary-looking building. But only when you're on your way somewhere else. Not when you're trudging up the steps, past the massive concrete Xs and the huge slabby pillars with the emblem banged onto them, and then under the sign with the pointy blue logo, through the doors into the glary reception, and saying to the constable behind the glass, "Uh—I'd like to confess to a crime, please?"

Pretty quickly I ended up in a sixth-floor room with a constable, whose name I forgot as soon as she said it. I was freezing. My jaw felt locked and achy. Every time I talked—even just a couple of words—my voice made random leaps and wobbles.

It wasn't that the constable was threatening. Apart from the matter-of-fact bollocking she gave me at the start, when she said I'd done an idiotic, bone-headed thing and where had I parked my brains and a few other things like that, she was almost kindly.

The room had white tables and red chairs, and a whiteboard at one end, and windows that looked out onto another massive concrete building. Pigeons kept flapping clumsily past the windows or crash-landing on the white-spattered ledges opposite.

Mostly I tried to keep my eyes from going plate-sized, which they kept doing when I didn't pay attention. And particularly when the constable said she'd have to ring Mum.

She phoned from an office next to the interview room. I could see her through the window, shifting in her roller chair, but I couldn't hear what she was saying—I just saw her hand slowly waving a pen, like she was conducting an orchestra. She turned once or twice to glance at me. Then she hung up and pushed back through the door. "She's on her way."

She left me in the room with a pile of gingernuts on a saucer and a plastic cup of water, and went back next door.

It gave me plenty of time to think.

Just say Celia was wavering—wondering if maybe she could send me and Fen to the same foster place. To some nice family who were desperate for a couple of brothers to look after.

Last night's doings would change her mind in a flash.

Plus, the car thing would be ammunition for the reporter. He could write another exciting article.

I kept picturing a prison cell.

Then the lift pinged.

I didn't let it show, but I don't think I've ever been happier to see Mum. I let her hug me for quite a bit longer than usual.

The constable read me my rights, which was truly strange. I got shaky and sweaty and my jaw went weird again. Then she interviewed me.

It was surreal. Attila, I found myself thinking, would have been very impressed. She asked me to describe very carefully what I'd done. And she asked a lot of questions. A few times she asked the same question a different way, which I figured was her sneaky way of checking up on me.

Mum kept offering me mints from the little red tin she keeps in her bag. She held it out again and again, when I'd said ten times I didn't want any. Every time she asked, she put her hand on my arm and squeezed.

At some point I dredged up the courage to ask the thing uppermost in my mind. "Am I—is this—like, will I go, ah, to *jai*—?"

The constable tapped her pen against a knuckle, watching me. "I gather this is your first offence. And out of character."

Mum nodded hard enough for her head to fall off. *Her* eyes were like plates. The constable looked around the room, and sighed. "We try to keep this kind of thing out of the courts. If at all possible."

No one said anything. Then Mum said faintly, "So … ?"

"So," said the constable, giving me a cautionary frown, "it's unlikely you'll be going to jail."

That's when I started to really sweat and shake.

Which makes no sense at all.

Gobhead Next Door

The more the constable went on about ordinary, everyday things like meetings and times and dates, the more unreal it all seemed.

She mentioned Youth Services. And a thing called a family group conference. One time she described Boyd as "the victim", which gripped my attention for a few seconds. But in general, it was hard to get my head around it all. I nodded a lot.

It didn't help that phones were ringing endlessly and people tromping back and forth in the main office.

Mum said something. After a few seconds it registered: "You'll have to tell ... Boyd?"

The constable started slapping everything into a folder, page by page. "That's right. We'll give him a call. Take him through the process." She closed the folder, sat back and looked from Mum to me. "After a confession like this—" she tapped the folder— "policy is, we invite the victim to attend the family group conference." She paused. "Same time as we inform them of the perpetrator's name."

I glanced at Mum, and she glanced at me. I felt sick.

"How ... ah, how soon?" said Mum.

"Hard to say. Just now, meetings are running ... a month or two out."

Next door, the constable's phone started ringing.

I needed to ask when exactly they would tell Boyd.

But, maddeningly, she was talking again. "One other thing. Should've mentioned it. The usual deal is, the perpetrator pays for damages."

Somehow it hadn't even crossed my mind. I glanced again at Mum, and she glanced again at me. Now she looked sick.

How was this fair? Boyd had started the whole thing. I tried to calm down, but it was too late.

"What about the damages to my brother?"

Saying it only made me angrier. "The damages," I said louder, "caused by gobhead next door?"

The constable looked mildly surprised.

"Driving straight at us in the idiot-mobile?" I shot forward in my chair. "With Dozo Derek egging him on at a million miles an hour?" I was at full volume. Out in the middle office, a couple of people looked over. I finished in an embarrassed mutter. "What about those damages?"

The phone stopped ringing.

Mum was staring at me.

The constable folded her arms and leaned back in her chair. "Gobhead next door?"

No one answered.

"I'd hazard a guess that would be Boyd?"

I nodded, feeling bleak. The constable shuffled a couple of pages. She picked up her pen, opened the folder and looked across.

"I'd suggest we take some notes about this."

"So," she said, maybe twenty minutes later. "I think we're all good here." She stood and came around the desk. "You're free to go."

I still needed to ask: when would they tell Boyd? But her phone was ringing again. "You'll be hearing from us," she said. I couldn't tell from her face if that was good or bad.

Going down in the lift, I thought, Here we go.

But Mum didn't say anything. Nothing, all the way home.

At our place, Boyd's car was gone. I sat looking at the mottled plastic of the glovebox, wondering distantly what would happen next. Mum clicked her door open and I smelled wet leaves.

Finally, she said something. "Tuttle. What were you thinking?"

I looked over. Her eyes were teary but somehow, in a weak, tired way she was laughing. She grabbed my shoulders. "You've learnt something? Yes? *Yes?*"

I nodded quite a few times. I must have looked worried, because she let go with a bleary smile. "You'd better have. That's ten years gone off my life."

Strangely, I was perilously close to bawling myself. I studied the glovebox door, following all the lines and blobs.

Plenty of ways of saying it went through my head, but none of them was right. Finally it came out when I didn't mean it to, and louder than I expected. "Were you going to just let Celia tell us?"

She sounded puzzled. "Tell you what?"

"Fostering. I heard you on the phone to Aunty Sally."

She leaned right back to focus on me, looking horrified. "Oh, no. Did you think—you thought you were being fostered out?"

"Well? Aren't we?" But even while I said it, I was thinking, Wait. This suggests otherwise.

"*No*," said Mum. "No, no, *no!*" She threw her hands around, banging the steering wheel. "You are not," she said, and dimly I noticed I was nodding again. Mum grabbed me by the sweatshirt and shook. "D'you hear me? You're not!"

"Fine," I said. "Jeez." I couldn't help grinning.

Mum had been quiet for a while.

"It's my fault," she said. "My fault you went off the rails. The article was right, I wasn't managing. You had to help Fen. Make meals. Vacuum. Of course you lost it. There was no one there to help you through it, no one to—"

"Nah," I said. "I can stuff things up pretty well all by myself." A crafty thought occurred to me. "But y'know, if you feel like doing the vacuuming and stuff for the next few decades ..."

"Don't push it." She ratted up my hair, smiling.

After a while she said, "What you heard. It must've been me telling Sally you *weren't* being taken away." She paused. "And how awful it would've been if you were. I couldn't have stood it."

She biffed my arm. "Crazy kid. You've always had a wild imagination."

"Not me. That's Fen."

"Uh huh. Anyway. Celia came here to say she'd talked to Fen's teacher, and one or two parents. And," she smacked the steering wheel, "she hadn't heard anything that couldn't be sorted out with a few sessions of counselling."

She looked triumphant. "Well. Since Fen and I've been seeing the counsellor for the past month or so—" she saw my face— "yes, we have, you made it very obvious you weren't interested after the first time ... so. You are not being fostered out. Is that clear?"

I nodded. Again.

Mum looked across at next door. "I can't believe he did that. Little toerag. Keep right away from him—and from his car."

177

"Suits me."

Someone must have put out bread crusts. I could hear ecstatic cheeping. "You know you can change your mind," Mum said. "About the counselling."

I didn't answer.

"It's been helping me with the guilt."

It seemed like six months ago, Mum saying it was her fault about Dad and Stephen Pritcher.

"Do you really think Dad would've done something he didn't agree with?" I said.

She looked surprised.

"Just because you told him to?"

She looked more surprised. Thunderstruck, even.

"Anyway. No thanks. The counselling, I mean."

Mum didn't say anything for a long time.

Then she crossed her arms over the steering wheel, dropped her chin onto them, and did a long sigh.

"Here's an idea. We go in. We make toast. And hot chocolate for Fen, if he's awake. Then we turn on the TV and sit on the couch and watch something mind-numbingly trashy."

We found an Australian dating show that was perfect.

Comet Brew

Fen fell asleep on the couch five minutes into the show. Mum pulled a blanket over him and lowered the sound on the TV, and we watched to the bitter end.

The credits started flashing.

"Try to get some sleep," said Mum.

I reached my arms up the wall behind me. Nothing seemed real. The day was stretching out, longer and longer. I couldn't believe it was only twelve hours since I'd gone after the car.

"Sleep," said Mum, louder. "We'll have a late lunch."

I wondered what was happening at school. What Attila was thinking.

"I'll tell Fen about the car," said Mum. "Now, bed."

From my room I checked next door. Still no sign of the car. They must have had it towed.

It was pointless trying to sleep. I fiddled around with website designs, but couldn't concentrate for more than ten seconds at a time. I kept remembering the chisel, and the shiny paintwork and blobs of dew. And wondering when the police would ring Boyd for their little chat.

Mum stamped up the hallway and started an annoying rummaging in the cupboard. She pulled something out with a crash and a "Ha!" and thumped away again, and everything went quiet except for the whoosh of running water.

Then a door banged and Mum yelled, "Take that, you stupid cat!" and I heard a yowl, and outside Figaro made a flying bound over the fence.

When I got to the living room, Mum was cradling the super-soaker and staring commando-like out the french doors.

"What's going on?" I said.

"Figaro," said Mum. "Doing his business. Right in the lavender."

I frowned. "Cats do that. He doesn't know."

"He'll learn. He's a lot smarter than he lets on—it's all an act with him." She tapped the super-soaker. "Here's the lesson plan."

Her face had pink in it. You could almost see the nervy, rocket-around person she used to be. I felt bad for Figaro, but it was true—he was smart. He'd have to ride this one out.

We had lunch, which was weird because it was mid-afternoon, and I kept catching Fen staring at me with round eyes. Mum must have told him.

Attila finally came online around four o'clock.

Zeustian Logic: Hey.

Tacky Psi Arm: ha. long time no say

Zeustian Logic: Yeah. Sorry.

Tacky Psi Arm: sorry for being jerk of the century?
    or sorry for not getting online a HELL of a lot sooner?

Zeustian Logic: Yeah. That.

Tacky Psi Arm: quite all right

> no problemo compadre
>
> BUT where the hell were you today
>
> **Zeustian Logic:** Long story. See you tomorrow?
>
> **Tacky Psi Arm:** why not today?
>
> **Zeustian Logic:** Stuck here.

I didn't mention that I was grounded. ("Resting. Until at least Monday.") But I was hopeful of wheedling my way around it.

> **Zeustian Logic:** I'll try for tomorrow.
>
> **Tacky Psi Arm:** & i will reveal progress with the non-chosen novel
>
> wait.
>
> factor in my saturday beauty sleep

I went out to the shed step, to sort through the crate of beer stuff. I'd decided to make ginger beer. The idea had been brewing for a while. (Ha. One day I'll out-Attila Attila.)

It felt pretty good, sorting things out with him.

I got a bucket and scrubbing brush, and dragged the hose out onto the lawn to start washing bottles. They glinted in the sunny patches between long tree shadows. I could hear and occasionally see Figaro in the lavender, his long body slipping past the stems.

Mum bustled out the front door with Fen in tow. He spotted Figaro and rushed across the lawn, and Mum yelled, "Three minutes. Max." She came over.

"Oh. Comet Brew. That takes me back. He named it after you, do you remember?"

I shook my head, and she settled on the grass.

"You were six or seven. You'd been begging for weeks to help with beer-making. Finally Dad let you do a batch. And he liked the name so much he made it official." She snorted. "He said it was fitting—no matter what he tried, the head on the beer always looked like a dirty snowball."

Fen had crept right into the shrubbery after Figaro. "Time's up," Mum called.

They went off for their counselling session, but not before Mum had reminded me to keep right away from Boyd. She even tried to get me to go inside—to cower behind the curtains, I suppose.

When they'd left I went back to swilling out bottles.

I was scraping with the brush, just mulling everything over, when it sank in that for the last ten seconds or so I'd been hearing Boyd's car careening through the streets, getting closer.

I went out on the lawn to look.

The car squealed around the corner at the end of our street and kept up the speed till the last possible second, when it slid into next door's driveway. The tyres thumped—front left, rear left.

He'd got those replaced, then.

The driver's window was taped up with wrinkled plastic, with a blur of orange hair behind it.

I took in the rest of the damage. There were still scrapes along the side panels—long lines with dark metal showing, mostly straight but with the occasional curve. Below the driver's window the red was pocked with scars from brick and glass.

But now the door was open and Boyd was out, yelling and taking huge strides across the grass towards our fence.

Derek the Dragonslayer

Derek launched himself out the passenger door, yelling too.

I stood half-bent and blinking. I knew what was going to happen.

Boyd barely noticed the fence. He clobber-climbed it and landed. Whatever he was shouting, it didn't make sense. He rushed the last few steps, his face a grimace with spit flying off it, while I tried to figure out how to move.

I wasn't quick enough. He barged into me, shoving and thumping with fists, elbows, arms and chest. I basically flew onto the grass—that's the trouble with having a frame that's average or slightly less—and bounced.

He was there again in an instant, hanging over me. His face was dark red. "You'll wish you'd—" He stopped making sense again.

My own face was on the ground by then, so I didn't see the kicks coming for my legs, ribs and belly. I felt them more as thuds than anything else.

I got my arms over my head and curled up, trying to get a breath. Boyd was still shouting, and the words were still garbled, but his meaning was clear enough.

I heard a thump that must have been Derek coming over the fence. In a disconnected way I thought, Here we go, two of them. But it got me moving. I flipped over into a crab stance on my hands and heels, scrambling backwards and trying to get up.

Boyd followed. His foot went back for another kick. Behind him, Derek ran three or four long steps.

But, unbelievably, he snagged Boyd's arm and hauled him around, away from me. "Hold up."

Boyd twisted back, dragging Derek. In another second they were almost on top of me. Derek got his footing and hooked an arm around Boyd. "C'mon," he yelled. "Y'can't—y'gotta—"

I was still on the ground, looking up, almost mesmerized. I remembered myself and scuttled back, then upright. Boyd's ginger-haired arms reached out at me.

"C'mon," Derek huffed. He glanced at me over Boyd's shoulder. They edged closer.

Boyd pulled out of his grip. I got in a couple of elbow swipes and a kick before his shoulder whacked the side of my head and all the sounds of squelching lawn and birds went muffled. He put me in a headlock, squeezing.

Derek grabbed again. Boyd let go, and I tottered back.

"Y'can't," said Derek. He shook Boyd. "It's assault."

Boyd stood breathing, watching me.

"Leave him. He'll pay," said Derek.

"Why'd you do it?" Boyd said.

For that second or two, he looked like a hurt little kid.

Then the old Boyd was back. It was almost a relief to see his sneer. I expected him to erupt again, and Derek obviously thought the same, because he edged forwards. "He'll pay. Police'll sort it."

"He'll pay, all right." Boyd jabbed a finger at me. "Every buck."

I looked at his finger. "They already told me."

He frowned.

"The police. When I told them I'd done it."

He exchanged a disbelieving look with Derek.

Then he leaned back and crossed his arms. "Well?"

I looked at Derek, but he seemed just as confused as I was. No one moved.

"Apology," Boyd snapped.

My forehead went hot. I went through a rapid reasoning process. I was already messed up. What was a bit more blood and bruising? I could barely feel it anyway—there wasn't much point in stopping now. So I said, "Why don't you apologize?"

Sometimes I wish I'd give these things more thought.

Boyd looked genuinely surprised.

I went closer. He had a lot more freckles than I'd realized.

"Why don't you?" I said again. "For all the crap you've said about me and my family? And for driving your—" I was too angry to think of anything really cutting— "moronic car at my brother?"

His expression turned into amazed delight, as if he couldn't believe the rare gift I'd given him. "Aw." He turned and punched Derek's arm. "Liddle bruvver."

"You both should," said Derek.

Boyd, who was already swinging back to me, did a double-take.

Derek looked calm. "Y'know. Say sorry. To each other."

I was staring too, by then.

Derek leaned forward. "They did research. They worked it out. They figured out that saying sorry makes people feel better." He lifted his hands, then dropped them. "Makes them happier. Gives them self-respect. Clears out the shame and guilt. All the stuff that makes them sick."

Boyd and I gaped.

"It makes them feel vulnerable," Derek went on, "and sort of closer to each other. And also, it's embarrassing to apologize." He shrugged. "So it makes people think twice about doing the same shitty old crap later."

"Bloody hell." Boyd didn't seem to know where to look. Then he remembered me. "Every last buck," he snarled.

"Fine by me," I said.

I had a plan.

George

I used the tea towel to wipe dirt and blood off my face.

Everything hurt. But there were things to do.

I'd had the brainwave when I was cleaning the Comet Brew bottle, just before Boyd turned up. If Mum could make money from wine and beer labels and logos, maybe I could raise a few dollars making websites. It'd be handy now there were car repairs to pay for. I started thinking about the sites I used every day. And that was when it hit me: the observatory.

Their website was already good. But there were a couple of things I could think of to make it … well, *primo*.

The trouble was, Mum and Fen would be home any minute. Unless—hadn't Mum said something about going to the super-market after the counselling?

I rushed into clean jeans and shirt, meanwhile going back and forth to the computer to open website layouts. I sent the best three to the printer, with different versions showing tabs and menus and social media options, then raced to Mum's room to get them off the machine.

It felt pretty bad leaving another note on the kitchen bench, but what choice did I have?

Back soon. Don't worry. All good. Really.

The receptionist at the observatory was new. She gave me a funny look when I limped in. But I didn't have time to stop—I went straight through to George's office.

A few minutes later, he looked up from my printouts.

"Social media."

He said it slowly, frowning, in a way that suggested he'd never used the two words together before. I nodded.

He looked relieved, and I got my first flicker of real hope.

"Quite right. We do need that."

Was it really so easy?

I'd just sneaked through our gate when the car turned in at the end of the street. They must have gone for groceries after all. The relief. I hobbled inside and screwed up the note I'd left for Mum, and when they came in a minute later I was in the kitchen working on an I-can-explain expression.

The next hour was noisy. I've never seen so much antiseptic cream, swabs and bandages in one place. It looked like a hospital had been turned upside down and shaken into our bathroom.

Next morning I had time to kill. No one robs Attila of his Saturday sleep-in.

Besides, I hadn't managed to get around Mum yet.

I planned to be quiet and restful all morning. I'd eat and drink everything offered, meekly. I wouldn't show pain. And Mum would see that it was unreasonable to stop me going to Attila's place for an hour or so.

I spent a while on the veranda, lounging in the sun even though it made my cuts prickle. From past experience, Boyd wouldn't be up for hours yet. Not that I thought he'd come after me again. I just didn't feel like seeing his sneery face.

A couple of tui started going crazy in the trees, flapping from branch to branch. Phoebe came out of next door's and went down the street. She didn't see me.

I decided to wait around at our gate, in case she came back.

I'd been out there for a while, looking around and feeling generally all right with the world, when I saw her off in the distance headed my way.

Jitters set in. I had to move away from the gate to stop my knee drum-rolling on it.

She walked closer. And closer. I lost my nerve, and started talking when she was halfway down the street. "Do you want to go to the new planetarium show?"

She didn't answer. She just kept getting closer. I panicked. "Probably not, right? I mean, after all the—y'know, you probably think I'm a moron, Boyd and everything, I just thought …"

She was coming closer every second, and still not answering. I thought of running into the house. But then she said, "Sorry?" and it turned out she hadn't heard a word. I repeated myself.

And she said, "Yeah. That'd be primo."

And then she sort of winced and put out her hand, and basically pretty much almost touched my cheek where it was all rasped and purple, and she frowned and said, "Bloody Boyd."

Bruises & Balldozers

"Get on with it," said Attila. "I'm dying here."

It was Sunday afternoon. All day Saturday, Mum stayed unyielding. She only relented when Attila rang up, late on Sunday morning, and said something—who knows what?—that charmed her. "What a nice boy," she said as she hung up.

I hared out the door before she could change her mind.

On the way to Attila's place I relived—several times—talking with Phoebe at our gate. It still seemed likely I'd wake up and discover none of it had happened.

I wouldn't tell Attila yet. I wasn't ready.

We'd had a snack (Attila: peanut butter, wasabi and maple syrup on toast, me: one bite of buttered toast, then nausea from watching him) and gone up to his room. He hitched his chair to the left, making room for the rocking chair, and tapped the keyboard. The start screen for Balldozers bloomed into view.

I chose Crane Vortex. Attila took Tractor Beamer.

I leaned back, gingerly, into the rocking chair. Attila glanced over. He nodded at my purple cheek and the long scrapes and bruises down my arms. "Pretty good."

I didn't try to hide my satisfaction. "Incredibly painful."

The spectacular nature of the bruises was full payback for how I'd got them. I'd even rolled my sleeves up, which is something I don't usually do (for reasons of average frame, etc.). For the moment, I didn't care.

"Just flesh wounds. Mum went ape, though. I had to beg her not to go next door and bite their heads off. Literally."

"Nice," said Attila absently.

I leaned further back.

"So?" he said. "I hear talk that it was you who trashed Boyd's car. And you take THIS LONG to get around here and explain?"

"I got busy."

"Uh huh?" This clearly wasn't good enough.

I shoved the draught stopper under the rocking-chair runner, and tried to think. Attila stared at me, his fingers poised over the keyboard. The swirly patterns of the screen reflected off his face. In a hushed voice he said, "It *was* you."

I nodded.

There was a moment of silence.

"You beauty!" he bellowed. He gripped me in a short but painful headlock, let go, thumped my arm twice (I yelled), shoved his fist in the air and gave a wild whoop.

His elbow, coming down, hit the keyboard and launched the game. I lunged for the arrow keys, and he started mashing the left of the keyboard.

"Well?" he grunted, clacking keys. "What was it like?"

I blew out a breath. "Impressive." I sent five wrecking balls, one after the other, into the enemy stronghold. "They rang Mum to come down."

"Ah," said Attila. "Hm."

I obliterated a street sweeper. "Then they interviewed me." Jabbing an arrow, I flopped back in the chair. "Except—the rights were all wrong."

"Hold up there." Attila froze the game and turned. "Back up. You know what you just said, right?"

I shrugged. "Every time the constable said things like, y'know, 'You have the right to remain silent,' all that stuff, well, then she'd say, 'Please explain to me, in your own words, what this means to you.'" I scowled. "Every time. If I'd been watching in a movie I'd've been annoyed as hell."

Attila nodded with feeling, showing the whites of his eyes. He restarted the game and crashed the "a" key, shooting a tractor beam into the enemy's combine harvester. It was sucked towards us, faster and faster, until it self-destructed in a spectacular spray of wheat. "Ha!" shouted Attila.

My own wrecking ball came hurtling back at me, spinning. It took tricky keywork to dodge it.

"So," said Attila, scowling in concentration. "What's next?"

I sighed. "A meeting. With the victim." I sent a wrecking ball whirling into one of the enemy's warehouses and took a moment to enjoy the mayhem. Attila grunted again.

I swung the crane. "Gotta talk about paying, for one thing. Repairs." An explosion flared on the screen, and one of our silos started crumbling. Attila hammered keys.

It was no good. Our biggest factory exploded. I hit the up and down arrows together to initiate the vortex. Attila was banging keys continuously. His voice came out through clenched teeth. "How're you supposed to pay? Get a job?"

I stopped for a second, grinning, remembering yesterday's stroke of genius.

"Keep going!" yelled Attila. "What're you—we're—my health —crap!"

The vortex glowed green to show it was ready. I launched it at the enemy stronghold. It missed. "Aw, jeez." I dropped the crane at hyperspeed, ducking a cube of compacted silage.

Attila hissed and triggered the tractor beam. He was on low health—it fizzled and died. "No way," he muttered.

The enemy's combine harvester shot out a massive ball of blazing hay.

"No!" howled Attila.

It streaked, straight and deadly, into our stronghold.

Attila threw his hands off the keyboard and rocked back in disgust.

I waited for the sting of loss to subside and gave him my news. "I'm now, officially, social media consultant for the Bentham Observatory."

He turned right around to stare at me. "How the hell?"

"Long story short. I persuaded George they need my services."

He didn't say anything. Just kept staring.

I couldn't help grinning. "I'm a working man."

I think he was impressed.

Fellowship of the
Soulless FangMen

It was strange being back at school. Everything looked different.

Also, I couldn't help hobbling like an old hermit.

But the shambling—and the occasional groan when I knocked one of my bruises—just added to my reputation. The guys kept coming over in ones and twos, and smacking me on the less bruised of my arms.

In a good way, obviously.

In English it was crunch time.

MRS ZIEGLER [LEANS, STRAIGHT-ARMED, ON DESK.
    LOOKS SLOWLY AROUND CLASSROOM]: Now. Each
    of you, with the exception of Tuttle who
    has a week's extension, should be, to all
    intents and purposes, <u>finished</u> with your
    Chosen Novel report. [NARROWS EYES] Anyone
    who'd like me to cast a final eye over
    theirs, see me <u>now</u>.

CLASS RUSTLES, MURMURS.

ATTILA [OVER NOISE]: We can analyze Fellowship
now, yes?

MRS ZIEGLER [SWIPES HAND THROUGH HAIR]:
Patience, Patrick.

ATTILA [IMPATIENT]: I _have_ been patient.
You've had it for _days_. [PAUSES] A day.

MRS ZIEGLER [APPEARS SHIFTY]: I've not finished
reading.

ATTILA [SPREADS ARMS WIDE. GAZES AROUND]:
Everyone else has finished it. [STARES AT ME]
Almost everyone.

CLASS MUTTERS AGREEMENT, SWELLS INTO
DISCUSSION.

MRS ZIEGLER [RAISES HANDS]: Enough. We'll get
to the soulful ones, all in good time.

CLASS [INTERJECTS VARIOUSLY]: Soulless.
Soulless FangMen. It's Soulless.

MRS ZIEGLER [SMILES GRIMLY]: Yes. Oh, yes.
[A MOMENT LATER, NARROWS EYES, SQUINTS
AT ATTILA]: Do I understand you to say that
Tuttle has not had the pleasure of reading
your—work?

ATTILA [AGGRIEVED]: Hell _yeah_.

MRS ZIEGLER: That'll do. [CONSIDERS] Tuttle.
[ADVANCES ACROSS CLASSROOM, DANGLING FROM
FINGER AND THUMB A THICK SHEAF OF PAPER]
Would you be so kind? [PLACES SHEAF ON
MY DESK] An excerpt, to give us a—taste?

ME: Huh?

195

Attila jiggled in his chair, scrabbled with a couple of books, clicked his pen, and sighed.

I opened the manuscript to a random page and started reading.

"Geddoff," snarled Yellowcur. "Whaddya think yer doin'?"

"Sorry, boss," yapped Nippy, the smallest and smartest of all the FangMen, who had a secret desire to be leader of the pack one day. "Saw a flea!"

The pack moved out. Nippy was last because of clearing everyone's tracks with his tail. Slantfang Red and Grayflank started arguing about who should go first, and soon the green grass of the savannah was covered with blood and hair and a tooth, which was slimy and dripping with gore and gristle.

"That's a nasty distemper you've got, Grayflank," said Nippy. "Geddit?"

Still they went on.

The bell rang.

"Texts away," said Mrs Ziegler. She stepped briskly around her desk, sweeping exercise books into her green satchel, and banged out the door. I looked at Attila, who shrugged.

Noise built up as guys knocked against desks and put stuff in their bags. A circle of devotees formed around us.

I went on.

Many gibbous moons and throaty howls later they came to Datey, the welcome oasis where they rested—

I stopped. "Datey? An oasis called *Datey*?"

Attila frowned. "Some of the names are placeholders."

I stared at him, and went back to reading.

—they came to Datey, *the welcome oasis where they rested and panted and fought like the fang-pups they once were.*

But it could not last forever.

"Move out!" slavered Yellowcur that next fateful morning. "Sandytown by nightfall!!"

I stopped again.

"Yeah, all right," said Attila. "You try coming up with fancy names every second word. It's not as easy as it sounds."

"Uh huh," I said.

Suddenly Slantfang Red howled with a sudden howl: "FLEE!"

Nippy whimpered. FangMen scattered with their tails between their legs.

Slantfang Red howled again, but with laughter this time.

"Got ya, Lamebrains!" he bayed. "FLEA! I meant FLEA!" He fell over from laughing so much, and Yellowcur cuffed him around the ear so that blood started spraying out. "I'll put a flea in yer ear," growled Yellowcur. "That'll teach ya."

"Sorry," whimpered Slantfang Red, but he wasn't.

"That part's great," I said. "I like that."

The guys all nodded and muttered agreement.

"Yeah?" said Attila. "Yeah?" He shuffled in his chair, going red. "It gets into a lot more battle stuff further on. You got one of the boring parts, pretty much."

"No, I like it," I said.

But he was right—it does get more exciting later on. It's

actually pretty hard to put down. On the way home, I asked if he was planning a sequel.

"Not a chance," he said. "Forget it."

But I thought he went kind of quiet after that.

Viator

I sat in the almost-dark with the flecks of stars, drawing the map.

The glasshouse was warm at first, and peaty-smelling from the soil mix Mum had patted into pots all afternoon. The glow from the computer was just enough to see by. I sat on a fruitbox and drew, and thought, and every now and then I stopped to look up through the ceiling.

It was tricky, getting the shape right.

When the basic sketch was done I went back over it, checking and reworking. Then I used some of Mum's old inks—cobalt blue, sepia and byzantium—to make the background. For the stars, I used one of her odds and ends of white pencil.

All in all, it took a couple of hours. But crap on high, as Attila would say, it came up all right.

Just for a minute, I imagined being a planetarium operator, showing it to an enraptured audience who were right on the edges of their seats. (As much as you can be on the edge of your seat, in a planetarium. Which isn't much.)

"Viator," I said to the invisible throng. "Centred on the star Canopus."

I leaned over to darken Canopus. "As you can see, Viator's not far from the Southern Cross—" I pointed with the pencil— "here."

In a moment of inspiration I remembered the laser pointer in the pocket of the computer bag. I rummaged for it, clicked it on and waved it over the map, making a blurry red swirl of the Southern Cross. Then I started around the surrounding constellations, one by one.

"Here's Canis Major, the Great Dog." I circled the dot around a big star. "See, that's Sirius. And just over here—" I leaned across to check on the computer, then took aim with the pointer— "you've got Lepus. The poor old Hare." I bent over the map to add a star I'd missed, and the brown paper crackled. "The Great Dog's snapping at its heels, apparently. If rabbits have heels."

I've always felt a particular sympathy for Lepus.

"Now, over here—" I made loops with the pointer— "are Corvus the Raven, Crater the Cup and Hydra the Water Snake. And further over, Castor and Pollux. The Gemini brothers."

The potting table creaked under my elbow. "And here's Eridanus, the big river where Zeus chucked Phaethon the Dozo."

I looked across the map and aimed the pointer again. "Then, about the same distance away, there's Orion the Hunter."

I checked Betelgeuse and Bellatrix, and Rigel, and sat back, considering.

Of course I might be biased. But I reckon Viator—my addition to the night sky—fits in with the rest of them pretty bloody well.

When I'd mentioned the map to Attila, he suggested adding a black tortoise. "Y'know. Black Tortoise of the North. For continuity." We were at the war memorial at the time, and he was brandishing a pointed stick.

"Continuity with what? Your deranged mental processes?"

"Well," he said. "No offence, but I don't get what's so good about putting him near that—what d'you call it?—Carina constellation. He could do a lot better. What about Aquarius? Or Leo?" He made a sudden lunge forward with the stick.

"What's better about those?" I said. "Half the time he'd be below the horizon. You wouldn't even see him."

"Yeah, but—the Zodiac, y'know?" He sprang backwards with a hiss of breath. "That's gotta count. Good suburb?"

"Forget it." I was corralling seed-pod things into a pile on the bench and wondering if they'd be any good in a pea shooter. "This way he'll have Canopus for a lodestar."

Attila tossed the stick end-to-end, looking blank.

"All the space probes use it," I said. "Navigation aid. Every explorer needs one."

"If you say so."

I nodded, scrutinizing the pods. "Mind you. They've had a few notable glitches. Like Mariner 10, on the way to Venus and Mercury. It had a Canopus star tracker. The trouble was, flakes of paint kept peeling off the craft and floating around nearby, and the star tracker kept thinking they were bigger and better Canopuses and locking onto them."

Attila looked briefly sympathetic. Then he shrugged and raised his stick to shoulder level.

Earlier, walking up Rugby Street, he'd decided—randomly, as far as I could see—to take up fencing. The sword kind. That, he said, or javelin.

He squinted along the stick.

"For a while there," I said, "it was happening ten times a week. They had to keep retracking. Wasted a lot of fuel."

"Ironic," said Attila. He launched the stick, javelin-wise, and watched its flight and bouncy touchdown. "All that tech, and the paint lets you down."

The glasshouse was getting cold. The ink was drying pretty well all the same.

In my head I wasn't a planetarium operator any more. The once-enthralled audience had drifted off. I tugged the sleeping bag closer.

"So. These stars here. They're the coiled-up rope." I traced the laser point from star to star, around the loops. "See, hanging off your left arm."

One of the curves had gone weird. I stopped to erase and redraw it, and squinted to check the new shape.

Through in the shed the old fridge hummed. I hoped the ginger beer was doing all right. I'd decided to call it Ursa-Ginga Brew. Out of respect for the Great Bear.

"Here—" I flicked the red dot across— "this is the belay clip." I paused. "And down here, that's your crampon. Fiddly. A lot of stars. A pain and a half." The problem, I saw, was all the spikes. It didn't need that many.

Canopus was great, I thought, as the hand-held GPS in Viator's hand. (Attila's idea—finally a useful suggestion.) "Then, out to the side, over here—" I touched the map— "that's your ice axe."

There were another couple of stars I could add in. In particular, an orange giant that'd be ideal for the sharp point.

"The axe," I said absently, studying the paper, "is in your right hand."

I pointed back the other way. "This, here, in your other hand. That's the rose, for Mum."

✱

There's something I figure Zeus never quite worked out.

You can get the world's most loyal dog, like Canis Major. Or the fastest hare, like Lepus. Or the greatest hunter, like Orion, or even the toughest warrior-scorpion, like Scorpius. Or maybe just someone who's pretty good-looking, like that shepherd Zeus turned into a drinks waiter. And you can shove them all up in the sky, like Zeus did in those stories—for being fast, or loyal or fierce.

Which is fine.

But there's other stuff, too.

Stuff that makes a person—well, just extremely impressive. Worthy of being in stories. Or whatever. That kind of thing.

And that's what I reckon Zeus never really got.

"See—the thing is," I said, and shifted around because the fruitbox wasn't the most comfortable seat. "The thing is."

It felt kind of awkward, saying it, but I wasn't going to stop. "The thing is," I said again, and finally got there, "I feel the same as I used to." I waved my arms, to explain it better. "About you. The same as I did— y'know. Before all the crap."

Then I hurried on, so things couldn't get slushy. "So. Well."

I looked down at the crinkled, shiny, dark-inked paper with the bright dots.

"Thing is, I made you a constellation." I did a big, dramatic swish of my hands over the map.

"And here it is. Viator the Explorer."

Mead Parties

The alarm cheeped at 3 a.m.

It was cold. The whole place was misted over, but up through the glass I saw a couple of feebly pale blobs. I zipped my jacket, got the map and went outside.

Everything was crisp and sharp-cut. Stars blinked. The intense black felt almost friendly, like a massive cocoon or a very big bear-hug. I could even start to understand Fen's obsession with getting his duvet swaddle just right. For a minute I got a soppy surge of affection for it all—the black sky and stars, the night air, the trees drooping over, even the bugs scratching in the dirt.

Something rustled in the lavender. Figaro's long shape flowed out from under the trees, and his flank rubbed against my legs. A faint meow came out of the dark. Then he wandered off again.

I held up the map, but— duh—couldn't see the drawing in the dark. I looked up instead.

Viator, the world's newest constellation, was straight overhead.

The map felt warm in my hands.

I pondered the sky. The extra star looked good on the ice axe.

Okay, so maybe at this point I should concede that the dozo counsellor didn't end up being a complete dozo.

But I'd just like to mention that I didn't write Dad a letter.

I drew him one.

With a clatter that almost killed me, the sunroom door opened and someone came out, shining a torch on my face. I squinted and raised my arm. The map crackled.

The beam tilted down, lighting the veranda boards. Mum whispered, "I heard you out here. What're you doing?" She came down the steps and onto the grass, which sounded crisp under her feet. I shuffled, and shrugged invisibly. "It's just … a constellation."

She shone the torch on the paper and came closer, directing the beam. In a slow, surprised voice she read, "Viator."

Things went quieter around us.

"It means explorer," I said. "It's … well, it's Dad."

Mum read the map, barely moving except that her other hand was on my arm and squeezing, and the torchlight on the page was wavering.

I pointed upward. "There."

She followed my finger and stared, then looked back at the paper, then back at the sky, breathing and looking.

"It sounds like 'w' at the beginning," I muttered. "Wiator."

I wished she'd say something.

The trees rattled in the wind. Mum was craning her neck. She did a wet-sounding sniff. "It's … just right."

But something didn't feel right yet. "Maybe I'll get Fen?"

Mum held out the torch. "He won't mind." She sniffed again. "Too bad if he does."

I went. The beam made crazy shapes on the grass and flashed on the sunroom door handle. Inside, I flicked off the torch and held my hands out on both sides. The hallway was black and closed-in, and warm.

It took three or four goes to wake Fen, me jiggling harder every time. Finally he sat straight up with his hair sticking out like a bird's nest. "What?"

"Come outside," I said. "Got something to show you."

He did mind. But he came. Complaining all the way.

I muffled the light with my palm and nudged him out the sunroom door ahead of me. His dressing gown hung crooked over his skinny shins and clumpy slippers. It looked weirdly short. He must have outgrown it months ago.

Mum was on the veranda, a dim shape among darker ones. "Come on." She put her arm around Fen's shoulders and coaxed him towards the steps.

On the second tread down he stopped. "I'm tired."

"I know. But you'll like this." They went out on the lawn, and Fen's high, sleepy voice complained again.

"Look what Tut's done," said Mum. Paper flapped. "Torch," she said. I went over and explained. Fen woke up a bit, and looked skyward through his sticking-up hair. He rubbed his eyes a few times and gave a faint smile.

We all watched the sky for a while. The trees leaned in over us.

"He'll make a name for himself," said Mum in a croaky voice. "Viator. Brewing beer."

Beer—I hadn't thought of it. "Mead. In all the stories they drink mead."

"Oh," she said. "Mead parties, then."

Fen looked back and forth between us.

"He'll do new varieties," I said. "He'll be so into it."

Mum snorted. "He'll be utterly tactless. Telling them all what to do." There was a pause, and she sniffed again.

Fen leaned against her and yawned.

The stars wheeled a bit more. A night bug chirped.

"Yeah," I said. "He'll sort them out."

Acknowledgements

This story has been a long time in the making, and has greatly benefited from writing conversations with Stuart Baker, Colin Basterfield, Nan Blanchard, Sarah Connor, Rachel Cookson, Ruth Corkill, Sacha Cotter, Maureen Crisp, Jo Foster, Lindsay Garnock-Jones, Elspeth Graham, Kirsten Gregory, Mel Hargaden, Patrick Hunn, Johanna Knox, Maryanne Martin, Christy Menzies, Penelope Newman, Shirley Phillips, Cheryl Rivers, Ceridwyn Roberts and Rae Varcoe.

I am especially indebted to Fleur Beale, Kate De Goldi, Craig Gamble, Mandy Hager, Eirlys Hunter, Elizabeth Knox, Abby Letteri, Kathy Taylor, and the late, much missed Mal Peet, who were all extremely generous with their time and writing advice. Fleur Beale has also formally mentored me via the NZSA Mentor Programme, for which I am very grateful.

For specialist and practical help, many thanks to Amanda Barclay, Dianne and Peter Beatson of the Foxton Beach house, Diana Burton, Heidi Drew, Noel Dunlop, Casey Garnock-Jones, Ian Griffin, Suze Kelly of Adventure Consultants, Simon Perris of Victoria University of Wellington, and Kim Tattersall, HoD Languages at Wellington College. Any technical inaccuracies are mine.

It was a privilege to work with editor Jane Parkin, who improved the story with great expertise and tact, and with designers Katrina Duncan and Greg Simpson, both of whose work I admire very much.

Particular thanks to the team at Gecko Press, especially Petra Westropp, Rachel Lawson and Julia Marshall. Rachel's and Julia's energy, perceptiveness and inspiration have made this a much better story. In addition, for years Julia has kindly encouraged me with this and other stories. Thank you.

Love and thanks to Nancy Malcolm, Bill Malcolm, Susan Archer, Mal Weston and Casey Garnock-Jones, and to Phil Garnock-Jones who, as always, has been a tower of strength and practical support.

This edition first published in 2017 by Gecko Press
PO Box 9335, Marion Square, Wellington 6141, New Zealand
info@geckopress.com

Text © Sabrina Malcolm 2017
© Gecko Press Ltd 2017

Distributed in New Zealand by Upstart Distribution, www.upstartpress.co.nz
Distributed in Australia by Scholastic Australia, www.scholastic.com.au
Distributed in the UK by Bounce Sales & Marketing, www.bouncemarketing.co.uk

Gecko Press acknowledges the generous support of Creative New Zealand

Cover by Greg Simpson
Edited by Jane Parkin
Text design and typesetting by Katrina Duncan
Printed in China by Everbest Printing Co. Ltd,
an accredited ISO 14001 & FSC certified printer

ISBN: 978-1-776571-38-3
Ebook available

For more curiously good books, visit www.geckopress.com